Thaddeus Grant Island Of Reconciliation

Book 1 in the series: Thaddeus Grant Island Of Reconciliation

A Novel

By

Phillip R. Evans

Published By Fulcrum Publishing

Author Notes

My inspiration for writing the book, Thaddeus Grant Island of
Reconciliation, came from life lessons. I have found myself on
the Bridge of Reconciliation quite often in my lifetime.
Restoring friendships or healing from pain of time past that have
come about by God's grace. Every time it happens, I envision
myself standing on a bridge with whomever has joined me,
leaning over the rail, and watching the fish in the stream below
swim by.
It's a peaceful time.

Whatever the issue was has passed into forgiveness. God's
word tells us that in order to be forgiven, we must forgive as
Christ forgave us. Forgiveness and healing can be restored on
the Bridge of Reconciliation by God's amazing grace.

I had a falling out with a friend, a brother in the Lord and we
were really close. The enemy broke the friendship for a few
years. Our lives went in different directions, and I missed my
friend. I shared it with God in prayer with hopes of restoring the
friendship knowing it would never be as it was; to be able to
fellowship and talk with him again as friends and brothers in
Christ Jesus.

Knocking on the door in prayer with the Lord for months for
a bridge of reconciliation, one night on Facebook the messenger
popped up with my friend's name. To be honest, I don't
remember who reached out first, but God had provided the grace
for us to be leaning over the rail in fellowship while watching
the fish in the stream below swim by.

God restored a friendship that I cherish by and through His
grace. I am a child of God, who loves my Lord Jesus.

Dedication

This book is dedicated to my savior Jesus the Christ, the Son of the Living God who healed me by his loving grace on the Bridge of Reconciliation, the Cross of Christ.

And to all those who seek reconciliation with others who have caused pain in their lives. It is not easy, but with God all things are possible. It is better to live in peace and have peace with one another than to stay trapped in a spiritual prison of pain of the past. The shame upon one's shoulders caused by others is not yours to bear. Forgive yourself and give the burden that weighs you down to the Lord and let him carry it. For he will, if you will, cast your cares and burdens on Him. Then watch and wait for the healing and peace he brings to your heart and spirit, to live life, for the one who gave his for you.

In order to be forgiven, we must forgive as Christ Jesus forgave us.

King James Version
Forbearing one another, and forgiving one another, if any man have a quarrel against any: even as Christ forgave you, so also *do* ye. Colossians 3:13

New Living Translation
Make allowance for each other's faults and forgive anyone who offends you. Remember, the Lord forgave you, so you must forgive others. Colossians 3:13

New International Version
Bear with each other and forgive one another if any of you has a grievance against someone. Forgive as the Lord forgave you. Colossians 3:13

REPENTANCE AND FAITH

"Dad, I had a dream about mom." He stood there with sad-ness on his face and his backpack on his back that carried a picture of his mom and his favorite authors' book he had just received.

Pastor Teetson looked at his sad son. He didn't know where his wife was. There had been an unexpected separation. The small church he was pastoring had shut its doors and closed leaving him without a flock. He was unable to find another church. Every door he tried was shut, he became frustrated feeling hopeless, and he lashed out with bitterness. *Why did God give me a church and then take it away and not open the door to another church congregation for me?*

His wife, Kathryn, would try to comfort him believing God had a plan. The Pastor's bitterness and frustration boiled over one day, and he and his wife had argued. She told him she was going to pray in the park where she would go for solace sometimes. When she returned her husband and son were gone!

A neighbor said that he left in a huff and puff quickly. She waited for three days trying to find them to no avail. No one knew where they were, and the authorities could not find them. He had been called away to help a family who was in desperate need and in his frustrated state he hadn't heard his wife say she was going to the park to pray. He hurried out of the house grabbing his son, letting the neighbor know he had a call to help a former member of the church that had closed. They didn't have a phone. When he realized he wouldn't be able to return home for a few days, he called his neighbor asking her to let his wife know he would be gone for a few days. She said, "I will.," but she didn't.

When he returned home his wife was gone. He fell to his knees remembering the attitude he had before he was called away. *What have I done?* He was sad holding his son in his arms hoping she would return, but she never did.

The Pastor asked his son, "What was the dream about?"

His son Randy replied, "I dream she was on a beautiful and peaceful island in a palace. Mom was crying and very sad, calling out for me and you. She was telling someone she was sorry, hoping and praying we would come home. I prayed to God crying that I wish I could see and be with my mom because I miss her and need her." Tears fell from Randy's eyes until he fell asleep.

Pastor Teetson placed his young son in his arms and began to cry. Holding his son in his arms, he prayed, "Father in heaven I am so sorry for the lack of faith, bitterness, and frustration that I showed to you and my wife Kathryn. I ask for forgiveness and for you to increase my faith. I know the island in my son's dream, and I have no doubt Kathryn is calling out to us. Please let us reunite our love and let us go home to the Island of Reconciliation."

The Pastor fell asleep with his son in his arms. When he awoke, he and his son were in the inland town of Harborshire.

Thaddeus Grant Island Of Reconciliation

Pastor Teetson woke his son out of his sleep. Randy, wiping away the sleep in his eyes said, "Dad where we at?"

His dad said, "We're in "Harborshire," he picked up Randy to carry him. "We must hurry to catch the Boat of Faith so we can go to the Island of Reconciliation to find your mom."

He hurried, seeing the elderly gentleman that use to give the tickets to ride the Boat of Faith. "Hello, we need two tickets to board the Boat of Faith to go to the Island of Reconciliation."

The older gentleman said to him, "The Boat of Faith? That has not been the entrance to the Island of Reconciliation for some time now, Matter of fact, years!"

Pastor Teetson said, "Then how do we get there?"

The elderly man said, "You can rent a carriage or take a step of faith but you both will need faith, both you and your son." He then pointed to the end of the harbor pier where there was only water beyond. "When you are ready to take your step of faith, or you can rent a carriage and it will be your ride of faith. Once you have arrived you will need to do an act of kindness. Let me find the ledger so I can see what kindness act you're required to do. I'll be right back."

The Pastor knelt to his son saying, "Randy we need to have the faith that you have, a child-like faith." He pointed to the end of the harbor pier where there was only water for as long as one could see.

Randy looked at his dad and said, "Can we rent a carriage? I've never ridden in one."

His dad smiled at him and said, "Yes."

Randy said, "Then let us take a ride of faith." A sparkle and gleam of excitement could be seen all over Randy's face as he began to sing, "Oh praise my Lord, my salvation, praise, praise, praise the Lord." His dad enjoined with him singing praise to the Lord. The more they sang the more their faith grew in the Lord.

The older gentleman found the ledger and remembered Randy's dad when he and his wife with their young child came to Harborshire years before. How his wife had tears in her eyes, was nice and kind, and how the boy who had fallen asleep crying and how his dad was abrupt and upset. He found the ledger looking through the pages finding the name Teetson column with the note: a mean and angry lot who bully.

Returning he said, "Mr. Teetson here is the kind act that you will need to do once you arrive on the Island of Reconciliation"

Randy was a very young eight-year-old and was small for his size. "Sir my dad is Pastor Teetson."

The older gentleman looked down at young Randy and said, "God works in mysterious ways." *Praise you Lord for answered prayer.* "Pastor Teetson your carriage rental is free today and I've given two of my best black horses who are gentle they know the way to your act of kindness for you once you have arrived on the Island of Reconciliation."

Pastor Teetson and Randy climbed into the carriage and said to the elderly gentleman, "Thank you kind sir, and may the Lord bless you for your kindness."

The horses began to pull the carriage into a gallop to the end of the pier when Pastor Teetson and Randy's eyes closed in prayer, praising the Lord and off they went. When they opened their eyes, they were on a bridge that was a beautiful reddish stone and the horses that were given to them were white as snow.

The elderly man had watched as they disappeared and knew they had the faith that was needed. Staring down at the ledger his eyes opened wide and he said, "oops!" In a small notation at the end of the Teetson's long lists of bullying was the note that stated: "Albert Teetson's name was changed to Mr. Albert Dumpling, and he became Pastor Dumpling should he come back there is no act of kindness needed only repentance and faith that would have brought him back to Harborshire and then the step of faith to cross the Bridge of Reconciliation."

Pastor Teetson and Randy were smiling with joy. Pastor Teetson then looked at the note given to him that had the act of kindness. A distressing concern came over him as he was to go to the family of his cousins; the Brackenshens manor, who were mean. Their children were the worst of bullies and even the Teetsons would not go near them. They had a streak of meanness and bullying but not on the level of the Brackenshens family. The Pastor decided he would not take his son who was filled with peace, joy, and a sweet kindness to others to have him endure such a hardship.

Randy had memories coming to him of an uncle named Terry who had two sons named Terry and Steven. He couldn't recollect where he had met them, but he remembered they were always mean and bullied him.

Pastor Teetson and Randy had crossed by faith to enter the Island of Reconciliation. The bridge was new to replace the boat of faith. The boat of faith had a drawback that was causing issues (wet issues). Some would say they had faith. If everyone on the boat had faith, then there were no issues. There were, however, those that said they had faith but didn't. The boat would start towards the island and those without faith noticed their part of the boat would vanish and the people would be in the water and those that had faith would waiver causing them all to be swimming back.

So, the Grant of the island praised the Lord and prayed earnestly for a way for those with faith to take a step of faith without obstacles to cause their faith to waiver. A bridge of faith was built to form a cross to bring those of faith across the Bridge of Reconciliation.

Those that came to the Island of Reconciliation who could not come to reconciliations with those here after a time would leave. They, however, would have to have faith to step on the bridge to go back to Harborshire or swim.

While on the bridge they would hear the Word of God, "Repent for the Kingdom of God is at hand. In order to be forgiven, you must forgive as the Lord forgave."

Some would come back and a lot, because of their pride, would swim to Harborshire. Those that couldn't swim got lessons from those they couldn't reconcile with, giving them more time to learn about grace and forgiveness.

Pastor Teetson and Randy continued their journey while viewing the beautiful scenery all around them. Letting the peace of reconciliation fill their hearts with a joyful noise unto the Lord.

MEMORIES

It was a brisk fall day, and a chilly 40-degree gusting wind had picked up. The leaves began to fall from the trees covering the ground and street. Pastor Teetson hadn't been back for a long time. So much that the Bridge of Reconciliation was new to him. His son Randy was amazed by the bridge and his dad could see it all over his face as his son's face as it was lit up with a smile of joy. Randy had never been to the Island of Reconciliation before today. (He was too young to remember that his dad, mom, and he had lived on the island before)

Pastor Teetson told him, "You'll see a lot of amazing sites on the island." as he smiled at his son.

Pastor Teetson had just turned onto Grant Manor Boulevard. The streets were lined with lamp posts and each one had to be lit nightly. The road was paved with reddish cobblestone. They were approaching the Grant Castle Estate and he said to Randy, "Here comes an amazing sight for you now."

He pulled the carriage over to the side of the road. Randy had just turned eight last month and his eyes lit up with amazement as he had never seen anything like it before. The entranceway was so amazing. In the world they lived in he had never seen anything close to what he was seeing.

Two towers stood twenty feet high. A stone wall of gray and blue standing ten feet tall with a wrought iron gate lined the boundary line. The road was cobblestone with cherry blossom trees with their pale pink-white flowers with a 4-foot space between each tree as it aligned the cobblestone roadway. The trees stopped at a stone bridge over a lake. The cobblestone roadway then split off into five directions, and the main roadway circled the courtyard that was lined with beautiful flowers. Beyond that was the manor house where a "Grant of the Manor" was to live.

The property around the manor was a wide space of gardens with fountains. The surrounding walkways were peaceful and a lovely sight to see. On back a way's apple trees grew the best-tasting apples he had ever tasted.

Pastor Teetson told his son, "Every Grant that has come after the first has added something to the Grant Castle Estates for improvement."

Randy asked, "Can we see it? Do they have a Castle? With every book written by Jackson Randolph there is always castle, palace, and a manor."

Pastor Teetsons was smiling because he was so glad to see his son happy, joyful, and ready for an adventure. Pastor Teetson said to his son, "There is a castle and a palace, but they are in different provinces on the Island of Reconciliation. As for being able to see them, I don't know? I don't know who the new Grant is now. Thaddeus Grant was the estate owner. I got word that he had passed on to be with the Lord a few years ago."

Pastor Teetson, when he heard of Thaddeus Grant's passing, wished he would have been able to see him before he had passed because he had messed things up again. Pastor Teetson wanted his son to know some history, just in case, others would say things.

"There have been five Grants counting the new one now. Ranulf Grant was the first Grant, he was wealthy. He fell in love with the Island and bought it; all of it. This whole Island belongs to the Grant Castle Estates. Ranulf, which means Shield Wolf, had a dream of land green and lush with trees that would be called the Island Reconciliation. He had the castle built. Bennett Grant was the second. Bennett means blessed and he was. He had the village built with a church with all the stores, shops, and smaller cottages. Alistair Grant was the third. Alistair means defender of mankind. He began to build the palace. He became ill and was unable to finish it. Alistair Grant had left the property to Thaddeus instead of his heirs. This didn't sit well with Alistair's family who never visited with Thaddeus. Thaddeus Grant was the fourth. He wasn't even 15 years old when he inherited the Grant Estate. He had just turned fourteen. Thaddeus means courage; heart of courage, and one who praises.

"Thaddeus Grant finished the palace, built the manor, and tore down the wooden bridge replacing it with the stone bridge. He found the original plans that the first Grant, Ranulf, had made that he had envisioned for the Island of Reconciliation along with all its customs and began to restore and build. When he first met Thaddeus Grant, he told his son I was a brat and all the kids we ran with were brats. We thought we were something when we were nothing. We picked on a boy who lived on the island. He ran with us until he grew tired of all the games, we played on him. I had hoped one day to see him again to apologize to him hoping he would forgive me.

"He went missing a few years ago and no one knows what happened to him. He had found his fortune and was very wealthy. When he went missing, it brought tears to Thaddeus Grant because the boy was dear to his heart. We were the ones that caused his family to move away when he used to live here, and he had a heart for Thaddeus Grant as well.

"I met your mom here, and I was jealous of the boy because your mom and he were friends. It took me a long time to accept that they were just friends. One day I was picking on your mom, giving her a hard time and the boy said leave her alone. 'she's, my friend.' Your mom smiled, and I pushed her to the ground. The boy knocked my butt to the ground and your Uncle Terry came running at the boy and the boy knocked your Uncle Terry to the ground as well.

The boy said, "You can pick on me, but you're not going to pick on my friend Kathryn, she's nice, and she doesn't deserve it and I won't have it."

"Your mom smiled, and we just sat there on the ground, stunned that the boy put us here. A few years later I married your mom and one day we had a tiff that turned into an argument, I treated your mom badly. The next morning Thaddeus Grant's butler, Benjamin, showed up at my door and informed me that Thaddeus wanted to see me.

"So I went, Thaddeus told me 'I am disappointed in you.' I didn't even know he cared about me. But come to find out he cared about everyone. Don't let anyone ever tell you Thaddeus wasn't a fine man. He took an interest in me and straightened me out. Oh, also on this part of the island is where Bennet Grant built the village with shops, places you can eat, and cottages where those on the island lived and attended church."

Pastor Teetson began again driving to his brother Terry's cottage. He let his son know that he was going to drop him off at his Uncle Terry's cottage while he went on his call in the next county.

His son immediately went numb and downcast asking "Why can't I just come with you? I don't want to stay with Uncle Terry and his sons, Terry, and Steven, they always picked on me and called me Rainey instead of my own name Randy. Please Dad can't I just come with you, please?"

"No, I'm sorry, but I have to go help a friend with a personal matter, you'll be ok, I'll talk with your Uncle Terry before I leave."

Randy began to stress out with fear grabbing a hold of him, "Just find mom, and see if I can stay with her while you're gone."

"Randy, I don't know where she is on the island, and I'm required to do this act of kindness first for when we came on the island. When I finish, I'll come back, and we'll find your mom together."

Pastor Teetson looked at his son and in seeing his sadness, tried to change the subject. "So, whose books are you reading now?"

Randy replied, "Jackson Randolph. He is my favorite author I have all his books and just got his latest one but haven't read it yet."

His dad was distraught over the sadness his son was feeling. "Randy, you know when we're feeling down, we can always go to Jesus in prayer to talk to him about it. Why don't you spend some time telling him how you feel about this and ask him to help you? You know God works in mysterious ways."

Randy said okay and began silently talking with Jesus. He had just accepted the Lord a month earlier when he turned eight years old and was baptized. He was on cloud nine that day; filled with overwhelming joy. But today he was in a valley of sadness.

"Father in Heaven, I need your help I don't want to stay at my uncle's house with my cousins. They're mean to me and nice when everyone else is around.

"Dad says you work in mysterious ways, could you do one of those mysterious ways for me? I can't stay at mom's house, and I would love to see her. It would be nice to stay somewhere nice. Where I wouldn't be picked on or bullied even worse, somewhere I would be protected and cared for until Dad came back for me. In Jesus's name."

"We're getting ready to pull into your uncle's driveway."

As they got out of the carriage Randy was immediately greeted by Terry and Steven "Hey Rainey"

"My name's Randy!"

"Ok Rainey."

"Dad, please?" His dad put his hand on his shoulder and pulled him closer to him trying to assure him it would be ok.

Pastor Teetson told his brother Terry that he would be back in a few hours and didn't want Randy being bullied by his cousins or him.

As the boys walked toward the house Terry said "Come on they are just boys having fun. You know, like when we were their age and had fun with Rudy" he began to laugh.

Pastor Teetson said, "It wasn't funny what we did to that kid and his name wasn't Rudy. I feel bad about how we all ganged up on him. Should the opportunity arise with a chance to see him again, I hope he will accept my apology."

Terry's response was with a smirking grin, "Not me. Don't owe the dweeb anything."

Pastor Teetson just shook his head and said to his brother "Terry you haven't changed at all. I'll continue to pray for you to understand how we treated that kid."

"Pray for me! I don't need your prayers and your holier than thou preaching," then followed it up with a matter-of-fact reply, "NO! I haven't changed."

Pastor Teetson was unsure about leaving his son with his brother, but he knew the family he was going to in the next county had kids that were ten times worse than his brothers.

"I'll be back in a few hours. I am entrusting my son with you to keep him safe and that means no bullying him." As he got in the carriage and drove off, he prayed silently for his son that he would be 'watched over and protected.'

Fearful And Frightful

ncle Terry didn't heed the request of his brother. As he walked in the house, he immediately saw his sons taunting and bullying his nephew. They called him Rainey, grabbed his back-pack, and played keep-away with it the entire time while laughing.

Uncle Terry said, "that's enough! Come on Randy, I'll show you where you'll be sleeping tonight."

"Uncle Terry."

"What?"

"I want to have my backpack back."

"Boys give him his backpack."

Steven threw it at him, "There you big baby."

They went upstairs and Uncle Terry opened the door to the boy's room. "The boys are sleeping over there on the bunk beds, and you can sleep on the mattress."

Randy went sheet white with fear, "Don't you have another room I can sleep in? They're going to bully me all night. Uncle Terry I know my dad had a talk with you about this."

"Oh! You want another room?" He picked up a pillow. "Come on, here's a room for you." He opened the door to the closet throwing the pillow inside. "That's where you'll be sleeping, go ahead step in." He pushed him in the closet shutting and locking the door. "Sleep tight!"

The room was tight and dark, Randy then realized his backpack was in the cousin's room. He tried to open the closet door and realized it was locked. He became frantic "Let me out, let me out!" and began to cry. The tears ran down his cheeks. "Why? Let me out!" He pounded on the door.

He could hear his uncle and cousins laughing on the other side of the door, finally, the door opened. Randy ran out only to be grabbed by the arm by Uncle Terry squeezing it hard pulling him back.

The boys walked by "You're in trouble now Rainey!"

With his uncle still squeezing his arm, he walked him briskly into the boy's room and yelled "There's your bed! This is a man's house we don't allow any crying in the house!"

Randy was scared. He was never ever talked to like this at home. He walked over to the bed noticing the mattress was wet and could only imagine what it was. His Uncle threw a mat at him. "Put that on the mattress."

His Uncle stormed out of the room. Randy fell to his knees, "Jesus why? Help me please!" With tears running down his face as he grabbed his backpack and held onto it while he pleaded with Jesus to help him.

After a while, his uncle yelled for him to come downstairs. He told the boys that he ordered some food for them before giving his son Terry the money. "I'm going down to the tavern with your Uncle Burt."

"Uncle Terry how long are you going to be gone?" Randy was at his breaking point.

"I'll be back when I'm back. You boys leave your cousin alone while I am gone."

It was early evening by this time and Terry and Steven said "It's ok Randy. We won't pick on you anymore. What do you have in the backpack that you are so protective of?"

"Just my clothes." He didn't want to tell them he had Jackson Randolph's latest book for fear they would do something with it.

"Well, listen we're getting ready to go, come on. What about the food?" Terry said. "We'll be back in time for it, come on let's go."

"Where are we going?"

"We're going to go get some apples at Grant Manor."

"Oh, ok I saw it on our way in it looks really cool."

"Just don't let old man Grant catch you cause some kids who have gone on the Grant Castle Estates have gone missing and never heard of again."

At eight years old, his cousins were a few years older than him. What they said scared him but being in their house scared him more. He thought maybe God was going to do one of those mysterious ways. He was going on fear and faith. Fear of being in their house and faith that God was going to do something amazing. His mom always told him "God has perfect timing for when he is ready to accomplish a plan He has put in motion. God's plan may come instantly or down the road while you walk your journey with Jesus. The time may be hard while in the steps, and you may not see what the plan is until God's perfect timing arrives for you to see the amazing grace of God's love,

He has in store for you. So just hold onto Jesus and keep the faith. Jesus will never leave nor forsake you."

They arrived at the Grant Manor. The Stonewall was too high to climb.

Steven said "Come on Randy, we know a secret way in."

They walked the stonewall boundary line until it became just a Wrought iron fence. Randy could see the Manor and thought it was amazing.

The fence was too high for Randy to climb, so his cousins picked him up and placed him on the other side of the fence. They were being so nice, and he didn't know why. There was a section of trees just on the other side of the fence, but you could still see the Manor. They began to walk through the tree area until it became an open area.

"Come on the apples are down this way." As they got closer to the apple trees the lights came on outside the manor, and they all froze.

The cousins started running back towards the tree line. Randy began running back as well. He stepped in a gopher hole and fell "He called out to his cousins to come to help him, but they just kept running and laughing, leaving him there all alone.

As they climbed back over the fence Steven said, "We need to go get dad and let him know what happened."

"What?" Terry replied, "Are you crazy you want to get your tail end whipped with the belt. We'll just tell him Randy got upset with a crying fit and left the house, and we don't know where he is at. I'm not going to get in trouble for that dweeb."

Randy was scared and alone, his ankle was hurting, and tears were falling from his eyes. He heard someone come out of the Manor and immediately lay down on the ground hoping he wouldn't be seen and that he could at some point make it to the trees. When he heard a rustle through the leaves of someone or something coming towards him, he tried to stay calm, but he was frozen with fear. What if they were right that kids went missing at the manor, he was hoping they were just trying to scare him. He was scared enough to be in their house so, he didn't need any more help with that.

As he lay there, he could feel someone patting his back, he raised up slowly with tears running down his face. Without looking up to see who it was, he said "I'm sorry for being on your property please don't hurt me."

He then sheepishly looked up and staring at him was a big St. Bernard dog who gave him a big lick across the face. Then he heard a voice "Phillip what you got down there?" Phillip, the St. Bernard, began barking. Ruff, ruff, ruff as he wagged his tail.

Randy looked back and saw a tall slender gentleman walking his way. He walked with confidence. He didn't look old, just somewhat old like his dad. The man leaned down "Looks like your friends ran off and left you."

Randy replied, "They're not my friends there my cousins." He began crying even more.

"Are you hurt?"

Randy replied, "Yes sir. It hurts from when I fell after stepping in the hole."

"Hey, there's no shame in crying when you are hurt, even Jesus wept."

"That's in the Bible. Everyone thought Lazarus had died, but Jesus said he was only sleeping and called for him to come out of the tomb, and he walked out in his grave clothes."

The man said "That's right! Jesus was crying because he loved Lazarus."

Randy then noticed someone else walking towards them, he wasn't tall, more on the plump side, but very jolly,

"What you got there Mr. Grant?"

Randy looked at the man and asked "You're not going to make me go missing, are you? My cousins said kids who come on the property go missing."

Mr. Grant looked at him with a smile and said, "No you're not going to be hurt, or go missing. I don't think Phillip would let anyone hurt you. He's pretty protective and if he has licked you across the face, you're a friend to him. I've never seen him lick your cousin's faces. He just chases them out of the yard. Well, it's pretty chilly out here. What's your name?"

"Randy."

"That's a really nice name, Randy. Let's get you up and see if you can stand on it ok?"

Randy stood up, but it was too painful to stand on. Mr. Grant then said, "Well you've got an important decision to make here young man."

"What?"

"Do you want a piggyback or a horsey back ride so we can get you out of the chill and send someone for your dad to come to get you?"

"My dad's not here he's in another county helping a friend, he's a Pastor. I am staying with my uncle Terry. He's mean."

"Well, let's get you in the Manor and then we'll see what can be done ok? So, Benji over here is the piggyback ride, and I am the horsey back ride."

Benji began laughing, "OK young laddie do you want to ride with this wonderful jolly Englishman or the Yank horsey?" Mr. Grant and Benji began laughing.

"I'll take a horsey ride. That won't hurt your feelings will it Mr. Benji?"

"No, lad, and it's just Benji, I am Mr. Grant's butler, driver, and chef. Mr. Grant and I have known each other since we were youngsters. When I needed help, he showed up and gave me a helping hand. He'll give you a helping hand now laddie."

"My name is Randy, not laddie."

Benji replied, "I know your name is Randy. Laddie isn't a replacement for your name it's what in my country we call young boys."

"Oh, I didn't know that."

"There is no bullying in the Grant Manor, you'll be addressed as Randy with respect. Mr. Grant, he doesn't like bullies."

MESSENGERS SENT OUT

The wind had picked up and the leaves began to dance in the wind which lightly picked them up off the ground. A drizzle of rain began to fall.

"Come on Benji, let's get Randy in the manor. Don't want him catching a cold in this chilly weather." The temperature had dropped a few more degrees.

Mr. Grant leaned down while Benji picked up Randy and put him on Mr. Grant's back.

Mr. Grant said "now we just have to get to the manor without stepping in any holes. We could get Benji to walk in front of us."

Benji looked over and stared at Mr. Grant, "Oh, so if we all fall, you'll have a jolly cushion to fall on." They all started laughing.

With the evening turning to nighttime outside, Randy couldn't get a better view of the Grant Manor. The drizzle of rain began to turn to rain harder as they rushed to the gateway and entered through a doorway near the tower that opened to a hallway. They turned right and walked a ways before entering a private room that was a study that Mr. Grant spent most of his time in. The room was large, towards the back was a spiral iron staircase.

Randy wondered where the staircase led. He had never been in a room like the one he was in now. Mr. Grant sat him down in a large, cushioned chair with an ottoman. As Benji put more wood on the fireplace, it began to warm them all up from the chill outside.

Benji helped Randy get his backpack off and offered to put it on the floor. Randy said he would like to keep it with him on his lap. Benji then helped him get his Jacket off and got him a blanket to put it on him to warm him.

The Jackson Randolph book that was inside his backpack was the last in a series that had been written. The book was hard to find because the writer hadn't published any books in a while. Randy was in awe as his eyes looked all around the room. He had only read about rooms like this in Jackson Randolph's books.

The Study was gray and blue stone like the front entrance with the gate. It had a large fireplace and stone mantle above engraved with *Trust in the Lord with all thine heart*. Tartan rugs covered the floor. Bookshelves adorned both walls on each side of the room, and a large desk could be seen. He saw chairs for guests to sit on and another door leading to another room.

Above the mantle was a picture of an older gentleman that he thought looked familiar to him. It showed two boys, one smaller one sitting in his lap and the other one with the older gentleman's arm around the boy.

Randy said, "who.... are they? The older gentleman with the two boys in the picture?"

Benji smiled and said, "That would be Thaddeus Grant and the boys are Mr. Grant and me. Thaddeus Grant is a fine man with integrity he is grand to be around and so many adventures."

Mr. Grant said, "Well let's take a look at your ankle." He untied and took Randy's shoe off, then his sock. The ankle had some swelling and was turning black and blue. "Can you move your toes?"

Randy was able to wiggle his toes so Mr. Grant thought it was likely it wasn't broken but thought there could still be a hairline fracture. "Benji, could you call for the guard to let them know we're going to need a messenger to get a message to Randy's uncle."

Randy's demeanor became sad when he heard his uncle was going to be called to the Manor. He worried he would have to return to his uncle's house.

Mr. Grant looked at him and could tell that he was sad. He informed him gently that because he was staying with his uncle, he would have to notify him of his whereabouts. "We don't want him to worry. Where's your uncle live? We'll send a messenger to give him the message where you are at."

Randy replied, "I don't know where he lives?"

Mr. Grant looking at him smiling said, "You don't know where your uncle lives, or you don't want to tell me?"

Randy replied, "No sir, really, I don't know! He's not there anyway! I don't want to go back there!" Tears began to fall from his eyes, "They're just going to bully me." Randy gripped his backpack holding onto it with sure fear.

When he moved Mr. Grant noticed the bruising on Randy's arm. With an alarming voice he asked Randy "Why didn't you tell us your arm was hurt in your fall?"

"I didn't hurt it when I fell. That's when Uncle Terry grabbed me at his house."

Benji returned with the messenger. seeing the black and blue bruising on his arm, he asked "Lad, did you do that too when you fell?"

Mr. Grant replied, "No, his Uncle did that to him. Send the messenger for my physician to see if they can come over to take a look at his ankle and his arm. Oh, and also find out what's the best way is to treat it until the physician arrives."

"Yes, Sir Mr. Grant I'll get on it and let you know" he hurried out of the room mumbling "What kind of person would do that to a child? Lord, protect that young lad he seems like a good boy."

Benji wrote the message and gave it to the messenger telling him "Take the message to Mr. Grant's physician and to hurry back.

Randy was tearing up. Mr. Grant leaned over to him gently "It's going to be ok. Do you know who the friend was that your dad was going to go help?"

"No sir."

"How long have you and your dad been on the Island of Reconciliation?"

"We arrived today"

Mr. Grant then knew because they hadn't gone directly to the palace that his Dad must have been given a kindness act requirement. "Randy, what is your Uncle's last name?"

Fear gripped Randy. He began shaking his head back and forth in signaling a no response. "I don't want to go back there!" Before Mr. Grant could assure him that he wasn't going to send him back to his Uncles house Randy said, "My cousins call me Rainey, that's not my name. Crying, he said "My names Randy.

They took my backpack away from me and played keep away and wouldn't give it back.

"Then when Uncle Terry came into the house, he told them to leave me alone and give me back my backpack. They threw it at me calling me a big baby. Uncle Terry then said, he was going to show me where I would be sleeping. We went upstairs and he opened the door to my cousin's room. They were going to be sleeping on the bunk beds and he informed me that I get the wet mattress.

"I told Uncle Terry that I knew my dad had talked to him about me not being bullied while I was here and ask nicely if he had another room that I could sleep in. He grabbed a pillow, walked me to the closet, threw the pillow in, then push me in, locking the door, so I couldn't get out. I wanted to get my backpack because it was in my cousin's room when I tried the door was locked.

"I kept asking to let me out. They were all laughing about it in the hall. When the door opened, I ran out, so I could get my backpack. Uncle Terry grabbed my arm walked me back into the boys' room and told me that was my bed and threw me a mat saying I could put that on the bed.

"He told me in this house there is no crying. I told him I want my dad to come to get me. He said my dad left me here with him and wouldn't be coming back for a few days when he was bringing back my new mom. I don't want a new mom. I've got a mom and I love her. Then he slammed the door and left. Later he called me to come downstairs and said that he ordered food for us and was going to the tavern with Uncle Burt."

Benji had walked back into the room to let Mr. Grant know the messenger had arrived. He had overheard Randy telling Mr. Grant everything and saw the tears stream down his little face.

Immediately Mr. Grant and Benji knew who the family was that Randy was talking about and most likely who Randy's dad was. Mr. Grant assured him that he wasn't going to be sending him back to his Uncle's house. "We'll send messengers out to find your dad and let him know when he gets back in town that he can pick you up here. OK?"

"Benji have the Commander of the Guard come to see me privately, but first tell me what my physician said."

Benji motioned for the messenger to come in with the message from the doctor. Mr. Grant looked back and saw it was Michael, a young boy at the age of ten. Mr. Grant greeted Michael "Hello Michael. What was the message from my physician?"

"The doctor told me he was ill and wouldn't be able to come, but he would send his new assistant who is a very qualified doctor and highly recommended. He wrote down the instructions on what to do. "The doctor is on another call, but he will send a messenger to let the doctor know to come to the Grant Manor. I gave the instructions to Benji. Will there be anything else Mr. Grant?"

Mr. Grant replied, "You can go and let the messengers know they will be going out tonight because we must find Randy's dad and let him know he is here and safe.

Michael replied, "We'll be ready when you need us, Mr. Grant." Michael could see Randy was downcast with sadness. "Randy?"

Randy looked up at Michael with sadness and said, "What?"

Michael looked at Mr. Grant asking, "Can I encourage Randy?"

Mr. Grant smiled and motioned his approval.

Michael knelt beside Randy whispering in his ear, "Be of good cheer, you are in a safe place. No harm will come to you here and you will receive a blessing while you are on the Island of Reconciliation. We will find your dad and give him the message and your mom knows that you are in safety and care." He then left the room.

Randy smiled and the sadness had left. He looked at Mr. Grant without telling him what was said. Mr. Grant smiled and said to him, "You are on the Island of Reconciliation and the messengers know why and who your reconciliation will be with."

Benji came back into the room. "I read the doctor's instruction. He said to put a thin damp cloth on the boy's ankle before applying ice, leave the ice on for 20 minutes but then remove it. This will need to be done every two hours, but the doctor should be here before then. He also said to elevate the lad's leg. He is to stay off of it and rest."

Benji said to Randy "I've got everything right here to take care of you lad. Let your tears flow as there is no shame in crying when you are hurt. Even Mr. Grant and my savior the Lord Jesus the Christ, the Son of the Living God wept.

"You're in the Grant Manor now! You'll be protected, and we won't let anyone hurt you. Now, let's get you taken care of."

Mr. Grant then excused himself before leaving the room to meet privately with the Commander of the Guard.

Daniel the Commander of the Guard approached, "Mr. Grant, you wanted to see me privately?"

"Yes, I will need for you to send the messengers out in all directions to find a Pastor Teetson to let him know his son Randy is at the Grant Manor. Send two guards with the messengers also. They just arrived at the Island of

Reconciliation today. They didn't report directly to the palace so, my guess is he is completing an act of kindness requirement. Let him finish it and let him know when he has finished it that he can come here to pick up his son. I also will need for you to have a guard report to the Estate Guards to pick up Terry Teetson and his two sons for hurting and abuse of a child."

When they were finished. Mr. Grant walked back down the hallway and disappeared into a hidden room.

5

TREASURE ROOM

M r. Grant had stepped into a hidden room that Thaddeus Grant had shown him when he returned to the Island of Reconciliation. The room was gray and blue stone and was behind another hidden door that led to the study that Randy and Benji were in at that moment. The room was large. There was a fireplace with a stone mantle above engraved with *For God so loved the world, that he gave his only begotten son, that whosoever believeth in him would not perish, but have everlasting life.*

Above the mantle was a shield with an R, a gold sword, three wolves, white, red, and gray together, and the shield was blue with a gold border. The shield had a nameplate but no name that had been filled in. A nameplate below was inscribed with the name Grant.

There was a large table in the center of the room with a wooden box sitting exactly in the middle of the table. It held the most precious gem that had been given to Thaddeus Grant. The table also had secret compartments that when opened would also open hidden compartments on the right and left walls. The floor was covered with a rug that was gray and blue with the same shield that was on the wall, On the back wall were four more shields.

The first shield for Ranulf Grant was black with a gold R and a crown, a border of orchid white and the R had a gray wolf on each side of the R. The second shield was for Bennet Grant. It was blueish silver with a cross. The third shield was for Alistair Grant. It was blueish gold with a cross. The fourth shield was for Thaddeus Grant, and it had a lion with a heart of courage holding a cross. The shield was white with a red border.

There was a large engraving in big bold letters that was between the four shields. It read "Thaddeus Grant's Treasure Room" It had a message written in a beautiful script lettering "My Treasure Room with my greatest treasure I had ever been given I leave to the Son I never had yet who was like a son I cherish with all my love, Jackson Randolph, who will carry on as the Grant Castle Estates Owner and all its lands and I give you also the name of Grant as it was given to me."

Mr. Grant sat down in Thaddeus's chair with tears rolling down his cheeks in despair. His head hung low in sadness and his heart was raced with panic. The numbness he had as a child was overwhelming him again as an adult.

Albert Teetson is Randy's dad and is a Pastor now. God works in mysterious ways. He was glad for Albert but also remembered he caused him to endure so much pain in his young life. The constant bullying from him and those that ran with him. He would always find the one that he felt was weak and use him as the pawn in all their games just so they could have a laugh.

The problem was he wasn't the first to cause Jackson Randolph pain. People hurt others in all different ways and

Jackson Randolph was already depressed before ever running with Albert and his cohorts only to become their pawn. His depression came from someone who was in the world. He told his parents of the shame he carried that wasn't his to carry but belonged to the one who caused it. They were able to come to Harborshire and then to the Island of Reconciliation. He could remember walking with depression, panic attacks, feelings of despair and hopelessness, anger, with no voice even though he could talk.

When Jackson returned to the Island of Reconciliation in secret with more pain than he had when he left, Thaddeus Grant leaped for joy because the boy who had become a man was like a son to him. He listened to Jackson Randolph and provided the Grant Manor for him to stay at. Benji who was his childhood friend was brought from England to be his Butler. He would go by the name Mr. Grant and everyone that was on staff knew who he was by name, keeping the secret that he was living in the Grant Manor as Mr. Grant.

The Grant Manor Guards were handpicked by him, he knew them when he was younger, and he had befriended all of them. Thaddeus Grant sent for Rich a counselor of God for him to talk with and by God's grace healing came into his life and he found his voice.

That night was the first time he had ever gone outside the Grant Manor. He sat in the tower and meditated on the word of God when he saw three boys come on the property heading for the apple trees. Benji had been working on some contraption that could light the outside of the manor while he was inside. The Grant Manor lit up outside causing all the boys to freeze like ice. Two of them thawed quicker than the little one with them and they began running. The little one fell down calling for their help, but they ran away laughing and all Jackson Randolph could think of was the little boy was their pawn in their game. So, he ventured outside for the first time since returning to the island to help Randy.

Mr. Grant turned back to the box that held the treasured gem. His mind drifted back to the day when he had told Thaddeus that he and his family would be moving away and that he was tired of all the games being played. He said he would miss him.

Thaddeus Grant gently put his arm around him pulling him closer and said "Jackson Randolph (his name while he visited with Thaddeus Grant at the estate) there are a lot of people when they are younger who are mean such as the Teetsons and their friends that when they grow up, they can change and be better than when they were younger. There are also some that don't grow up, remaining the same walking with meanness and hardened hearts.

"But I will tell you, you will return to the island one day and I know for a fact that you are going to meet a very special friend of mine, and you're going to become wonderful friends with him. If you trust my friend, he will help you to heal of all your sadness, he'll wipe away the tears. He'll strengthen you to walk in confidence with boldness to stand up and speak for my friend and yours. When the word is spoken, open your ears, wait for the softening of your heart. You'll be telling him your sorry, let your heart receive my friend and your life will change.

"On the days when you need him to come up alongside you, just ask for his help. For my friend has said, 'I will never leave thee, nor forsake thee.' Oh, and on the first day that you meet him, it's going to be a grand day. You'll walk across a bridge. The bridge is not made of gold or silver, no it is much more beautiful and precious than stones that man calls precious and much more valuable. It's a bridge that I call the Bridge of Reconciliation. You will be wrapped in His Father's grace of love.

"You'll begin to walk on a journey with your friend and mine and those who have caused you hurt and pain. You may find them walking with you on the Bridge of Reconciliation bringing healing to your souls that you can walk with peace that passes all understanding. Those that are mean, tell your new friend about them and do kind things for them. My friend told me 'it's like pouring hot coals on their head.' not literally, My butler Benjamin and his nephew Benji know my friend. My friend sent you on that first meeting with Benji when you were younger so you could protect him, and you did."

Mr. Grant came to know Thaddeus' friend much later in life, and he had helped him with things many times. His plans and steps were put in motion and were always on time to prosper him and not to hurt him and give him hope and a future.

Before he walked back out to the study where Benji and Randy were, he lifted the box to view Thaddeus Grant's precious gem, his worn Bible. It was ready to fall apart and had notes stuffed in every chapter. He just smiled with joy. As he walked out of the treasure room and into the study, Benji could tell his friend was ok, because he walked with confidence.

Mr. Grant asked, has the Doctor arrived yet? Benji said "No."

Benji quietly said, "You do know what family he belongs to don't you?"

Mr. Grant replied, "Yeah. It could all just be an elaborate game they have concocted." Mr. Grant and Benji prayed and asked the Father to show them the truth in Jesus's name."

Works In Mysterious Ways

"So, Randy I see Phillip hasn't left your side, as I told you he is very protective of his friends, aren't you boy" he patted Phillip's head.

Randy was just smiling and asked, "Mr. Grant "are you ok?"
"Yeah, I'm ok."

"When you left the room earlier you looked like me?" Mr. Grant looked at him questioningly "You look sad, I prayed for you."

The young boy had touched his heartstrings again, and he said, "Thank you. How are your ankle and arm doing? Let's take a look," The ankle looked the same. He was ready to call for Benji to come to take a look when Benji walked in

"Ok laddie, got you some cinnamon bread to tide you over while I cook us some of Mr. Grant's mum's pancakes. They're the best. Some bacon, ham, and eggs too." He looked at Randy's ankle. "Ah, the ankle looks a lot better the doctor will be here soon." He knew Mr. Grant was concerned.

Mr. Grant look back at Benji "That sounds pretty good."

"Oh, Mr. Grant would you like some eggs and bacon too." They both started to laugh and shook their heads.

Randy was smiling and said, to Mr. Grant, "I prayed the Lord would bless you as you have blessed me, you're my answer to my prayer today."

Mr. Grant looked at Randy, "Oh, what was your prayer if may ask?"

"After I told my dad I didn't want to go stay with my Uncle Terry cause my cousins always pick on me, my dad said, 'when we're feeling down, we can always go to Jesus in prayer and talk to him,' why don't you spend some time with him in prayer telling him how you feel about it? He said you know God works in mysterious ways.

"So, I prayed Father in heaven could you do one of those mysterious ways for me? I can't stay at mom's house, and I would love to see her. It would be nice to stay somewhere nice; where I wouldn't be picked on or bullied. Somewhere I would be protected and cared for until Dad came back for me. In Jesus's name.

"Well, Benji, Phillip, and you are my mysterious way answer to my prayer because I feel safe and protected here."

Mr. Grant replied, "Well you're a blessing to all of us here also. So, you prayed for me huh?"

Randy replied, "Yeah."

"Well give me your hand." Mr. Grant held onto Randy's hand and began to pray. Father in heaven you have blessed us today during this windy rain-filled chilly day with a blessing that has warmed our hearts. Father, I ask that you forgive us for our sin in our lives against you, Father I asked that you look down upon this child and bless his journey with your son. Protecting and guiding him into all your truths, not man's truth, but your truth. I ask that you grant him with wisdom that is far greater than the riches the world can offer, bring peace into his life and, your strength for the days ahead, for your confidence to stand for you, and the truth of your word. That those that have brought him pain and harm in his life to help him not to hold onto it. May he according to your will, and they that have caused him to hurt be able to step up on the Bridge of Reconciliation, the Cross of Christ Jesus to be restored with peace in their hearts. In Jesus's Name."

Randy reached up grabbed hold of Mr. Grant and gave him a big hug. With joyful tears he said, "Thank you!"

Mr. Grant reached into his pocket and pulled out a handkerchief giving it to Randy to wipe his tears.

Benji came in with the meal blubbering, "Ah, that prayer was so beautiful it reminded me of when Thaddeus Grant would touch our hearts with his prayers. Ah, Mr. Grant how come you don't ever pray like that for me, I would love to have a prayer blessing like that."

Mr. Grant replied, "How do you know I don't pray for you like that? I pray for you every night before going to sleep. You and the entire staff, and I always finish up the prayers for you asking that God would help you to not snore so loud. I can hear you all way down the hallway." They all began to laugh again.

Benji brought a tray over for Randy to place his meal on. "Randy, can you put your backpack on the floor, so I can put the tray in your lap so you can eat?"

"I want to keep my backpack with me."

"There must be something very special in your backpack that you don't want to part with it."

Benji and Mr. Grant both simultaneously said, "I can assure you Randy no one is going to take your backpack or what's in it."

"I have my mom's picture in a special compartment in my backpack, she's holding me, and an older man is standing there, I don't know who he is, but mom is smiling happily. I've also got a book in my backpack of my favorite author Jackson Randolph, it's the last one in a series he had written."

Mr. Grant couldn't reveal to him who he was. He was hiding there until the authorities could find who was involved in his disappearance.

Benji said, "Jackson Randolph is one of my favorite writers too. Would you like to see something I have that he had written? Let's eat our meals first before it's cold, and then I'll get it for you."

Randy let Benji put his backpack on the floor next to his chair. After eating their meals. Benji took the dishes and trays back to the kitchen and when he came back into the study, he was carrying Jackson Randolph's latest book that hadn't been published yet. Benji told, Randy that Jackson Randolph had written the book, *Jesus My Savior My Praise*, when he was struggling and needing God's guidance. Benji then handed the book to Randy and said, "Enjoy while I go clean up the dishes."

Randy opened the book to the first praise entitled "Whisper of Love." He looked up and saw Mr. Grant was becoming sad again. "Mr. Grant are you OK?"

Mr. Grant looked at Randy and smiled replying, "Yes, I am blessed because I have you here."

"Do you want to see my picture of my mom? I haven't seen her in a long time, and I miss her."

"I would be honored to see a picture of you and your mom."

Randy opened his backpack pulled out the picture and said, "I don't know who the older person is."

Mr. Grant looked at the picture and smiled. ""Kathryn!" before realizing he had said her name out loud.

Randy said, "You know my mom? Do you know where she is at? I miss her" Tears of love fell from his eyes.

"I knew your mom when I was younger. She was my friend and really nice. Doesn't your dad know where your mom is?"

"We know she lives on the island somewhere. We just don't know where. I dream she was on a beautiful and peaceful island in a palace. Mom was crying and very sad, calling out for me and dad. She was telling someone, she was sorry. She was hoping and praying we would come home. I told my dad that. I prayed to God crying that I wish I could see and be with my mom because I miss her and need her." Randy began crying again for his mom. "Then when we awakened. We were at Harborshire before we took a ride of faith on a carriage with black horses, but when we opened our eyes, we were on a bridge and the horses had changed to white as snow."

"If she is on the Island of Reconciliation Randy, I'll find her for you. That's a promise from me to you. Can I see the picture again, let me see if I recognized the older gentleman? I know him, his name is Wilford, if anyone knows where your mom is, Wilford will know."

Benji came into the room "Well did you read any of the book yet?"

Randy replied, "No. Mr. Grant knows my mom, and he promised to find her for me.

" His mom is Kathryn. I need to talk to Wilford." Mr. Grant asked if there were any more messengers available and if not to ask the commander of the guard to send a message to the palace for Wilford to come to the Manor.

Benji said, "I do believe all the messengers are out searching for Randy's dad. I'll take care of it."

"Randy?"

"Yes Mr. Grant."

Would you like for me to read to you *Whisper Of Love* by your favorite author?"

"Yes, sir."

Mr. Grant said to Randy, "Close your eyes and listen with your heart, letting the words bring comfort to you."

Randy said, "OK."

WHISPER OF LOVE

"I walked down an old country road, winding turns and gravel on the road, sunlight shining through the clouds, The road wasn't perfect, neither was I

I spent time talking to the Lord and listening, that's where I grew closer to Him. A cool breeze flows through the leaves of the trees, a small still voice, a whisper of love, I AM here, you're not alone.

I walked down the path for so long and came to many forks in the road, I didn't know which way to go, to the right or the left, just didn't know the way to go. A cool breeze flows through the leaves of the trees, a small still voice, a whisper of love, Don't go to the right or the left, keep walking on the straight and narrow path leading directly home to the open arms of my Love.

I lifted my eyes to the sky and saw a mountain standing so high. I didn't have the strength to climb. I bowed my head and lifted a prayer. A cool breeze flows through the leaves of the trees, a small still voice, a whisper of love. Turn your eyes to the Cross of Calvary, see the strength that was needed, my child.

I AM here, you're not alone. Keep walking on the straight and narrow path leading directly home to the open arms of my Love. Give me your hand and let me lead because you're valuable to me.
Jesus, I AM"

Randy said, "That was nice! I like that and the small still voice, that's when God is speaking to you."

"That's right!"

Benji came back into the room to let Mr. Grant know that a Guard has been sent to the palace with the message. "Randy, would you like for me to read the *Whisper Of Love* to you in the book?"

"Mr. Grant already did but he didn't read it, he sang it, he sings pretty well."

Benji said, "He's got some other good ones in there too."
Randy replied, "Let me look."

Mr. Grant and Benji smiled. They knew that God had answered their prayer to show them the truth that this boy was not playing in any game or was a pawn. They rejoiced! Breaking out in song together. "Lord, I know you answer our prayers we lift praise, praise, praise to you. You are our savior our King and you watch over me. Oh, Lord, we praise you."

Randy joined them and sang praise. "Oh Lord, You're my salvation, praise, praise, praise, you are my Lord of lords, my King of kings, praise you my Lord, thank you forevermore."

Michael sent word by one of the messengers that were looking for Pastor Teetson to go to the palace and inform them that a boy had been hurt and was at the Grant Manor. Thaddeus

Grant sent Wilford who selected two Estate guards to accompany him to the Grant Manor.

The guard that was sent with a message for Wilford to come to the Grant Manor met him on the way and gave him the message that Mr. Grant requested him to the Manor.

Wilford had arrived bringing with him a very special person whom he had met traveling on the road in her carriage. Daniel, the Commander of the Grant Manor guard notified them of the arrival of Wilford and the doctor.

THE DOCTOR ARRIVES

M r. Grant said, "I'll be back, I am going to greet them and let the doctor know of the situation." Mr. Grant walked out of the room making his way to the Great Hall to meet with the doctor to fill him in on the situation of abuse to the boy and to ask Wilford for the location of Kathryn?

The Commander of the Guard said that he had taken them to a private room to meet.

Mr. Grant said, "Thank you, Daniel." Mr. Grant then entered the private room he saw that the Doctor was a female who was chatting with Wilford.

Wilford said, "Mr. Grant" The doctor turned around. It was his childhood friend Kathryn. They both recognized each other and smiled and gave each other a hug.

"Wilford, I was just coming to ask, you where Kathryn was located on the Island of Reconciliation."

Wilford replied, "Oh well Mr. Grant she is right here for now." He giggled.

Kathryn said, "Why are you being called Mr. Grant and not by your name Jackson Randolph? What is the secrecy for?"

Jackson Randolph replied to her, "It is better for now, and I will ask that you not let anyone know I am here and to greet me by Mr. Grant."

Kathryn said, "Yes of course."

Mr. Grant said, "First let's sit down, so I can fill you in on your patient. Wilford, you will need to stay as well. The boy has been hurt and abused." They both looked very startled.

"He came on the grounds with two other boys, Benji was working on some new contraption to light up the manor from the inside. I was in the tower meditating on the word of God and saw the boys. When the outside Manor lit up, they all froze, the two older boys took off running and then the other boy, who was much smaller, began running also. He stepped in a gopher hole and fell down. He yelled for the other boys to come back and help him but, they continued running and laughing leaving the little boy there alone.

"First, his left ankle has some swelling, it's black and blue, he can wiggle his toes."

Kathryn said, "That is good it could just be a bad sprain."

Mr. Grant continued telling them what happened, "His Uncle abused him, he shared it all with me and Benji, Phillip was there as well. He has not left his side. He is on protected guard. His Uncle grabbed his arm so hard that it is black and blue. Our first thought was did you that when you fell and why didn't you tell us? He said that 'he didn't hurt it when he fell,' his Uncle did that, he's mean!

"We notified the Estate Guards about it and asked them to pick up the Uncle and the two boys. The Uncle did much more than physically abuse him. He also verbally and emotionally abused him in front of the other boys. I will let him tell all that was done because the more he can share it with trusted people who will not hurt him, the more he will be able to work through and heal. The little boy has been a blessing! He is very special, and I have grown very fond of him."

Mr. Grant bowed his head becoming overwhelmed. He said, "You both know the boy."

As tears fell from his eyes. Wilford said, "Jackson Randolph who is the boy?"

He turned to Kathryn and said, "I protected him and cared for him as you did me so many times. It is your son Randy."

Tears fell from Kathryn's eyes. "Randy? Jackson Randolph where is my son?"

"He is in my private Study with Benji and Phillip."

"Where is his dad?"

"Randy and Albert, Pastor Albert? Arrived at the Island of Reconciliation earlier today. Mr. Habens must have given him an act of kindness to complete. I have all the messengers that have been provided to me and my guards out searching for him and to let him know his son is here and to come to get him after he completes the required act of kindness. We don't know what it was. Randy doesn't know either."

"Oh no! He didn't leave Randy with Uncle Terry and his two sons, did he? What was he thinking?"

Mr. Grant said, "I will deal with Terry and his two sons. You should go to him now. He misses you and he heard your cry for him and his dad. Kathryn, you can't tell Randy my real name here on the Island of Reconciliation." Mr. Grant called for

Daniel to take Kathryn to his private study to take care of her son. "Wilford, do you know if Terry and his two sons have been picked up?"

Wilford replied, "I don't know. We have not received a report of this. My Commander of the Grant Manor Guard sent a guard to deliver the message to notify the Estates Guard."

After a while, Daniel returned to see if Mr. Grant needed anything else.

Mr. Grant said, "Did you send the guard to notify the Estates Guard to pick up Terry Teetson and his two sons?"

Daniel replied, "Yes sir, but he has not returned, and I am concerned because it is not like John to not come back after delivering a message. He is the youngest in our guard and takes the messages when there are no messengers to send, and I and the guards are concerned."

Mr. Grant asked, "Wilford, did you come over on a carriage or on a horse?"

Wilford replied, "A horse with two estate guards."

Mr. Grant said, "Where are they?"

Wilford looked at him and could see his concern and said, "May I ask why you want to know?"

Daniel just looked at Wilford with confusion and said abruptly, "Have you not just heard what I told Mr. Grant?"

Wilford looked at Daniel calmly.

Mr. Grant said, "Daniel, it's ok. Wilford never asks something without knowing the situation for the question. Wilford has just as much concern if not more than a Grant Manor guard has not returned, especially John, who he is very fond of."

Daniel replied, "I am sorry Wilford for speaking out of turn to you."

Wilford replied, "Daniel it's ok, I understand your concern there is no apology required from you."

Wilford said, "Mr. Grant doesn't have the authority to question the Estates Guard, even though the guard missing is a Grant Manor guard."

"No, I don't, but I know who does. Daniel, ready my carriage, two guards on the back of the carriage, two outrider guards in the front to make sure the way is clear, two in front of the carriage and twenty in the back split into two groups. Wilford notified Benji that you and I will be going to the palace. Have the staff return to care for our guests and return the guards to their positions until I return."

Wilford, replied "As you wish"

Daniel asked, "Mr. Grant may I accompany you."

Mr. Grant said, "If you come who will guard my guests and protect the staff and Manor."

Daniel replied, "Yes sir."

"Let Wilford know when everything is ready and one more thing detained the Estate Guards. Wilford, please let Randy know that I really cherished his company, and he was a great blessing to me. It's late have the staff prepare a room for Kathryn, Albert, and Randy for tonight and hopefully, I will be able to return in the morning. You will excuse me."

Mr. Grant left the room and Wilford smiled for now the GRANT was at the Manor that would succeed Thaddeus Grant.

Mom And Son Reunite

The Commander of the Guard reunited Mrs. Dumpling with her son Randy. Once Randy saw his mom come into the room his eyes let up with the love, he had in his heart for her and shouted "MOM!"

Randy said, "Mom, Mr. Grant said that he knew you when he was younger, that you were his friend and nice. He promised me he would find you."

Kathryn's tears were like a fountain overflowing with joy on seeing her son and holding him in her arms. She replied, "Yes, Mr. Grant and I were friends when we were younger. I am the doctor that was called to come to help you." She cried with joy that her son was now back with her, "Let me see your ankle."

Randy said, "Mr. Grant, Benji, and Phillip have been taking wonderful care of me."

His mom smiled and said, "I just had a very long talk with Mr. Grant. After I care for you, you and I are going to have a talk about what has happened." Dr. Dumpling looked at Randy's arm.

"Uncle Terry did that. He's mean."

Dr. Dumpling replied, "You haven't seen mean until I get a hold of your Uncle Terry. Hello Benji. Thank you for caring for my son." She patted Phillip on the head and "You too my old friend."

Phillip jumped up wagging his tail trying to put his head in her lap, she patted his head again with tears falling from her eyes.

Benji said, "Phillip let Kathryn be, so she can look after your friend Randy." Phillip barked "ruff, ruff," and then laid down next to the chair Randy was in.

Benji said, "Oh, Kathryn your son has been a blessing to Mr. Grant and me this evening."

Wilford came into the room and notified Benji that he and Mr. Grant would be going to the palace and that the staff was to be called back to the manor to care for the guest. Wilford also said that Mr. Grant said it is getting late and to have a room prepared for Kathryn, Albert, and Randy to stay for the night. He then turned to Randy and said, "Mr. Grant wanted me to tell you that he cherished his time with you, and you were a blessing. He hopes to return by morning."

Randy replied, "Is Mr. Grant, ok?"

Wilford replied," Yes, he has to go to the palace to remedy a situation there."

Randy said, "You're the man in the picture with my mom, who are you?"

Wilford replied, "Just an acquaintance of your mom and dad."

"Do you know when my dad's coming back? I am getting concerned for him, my dad is a pastor, and we came here to find mom so we could reunite our love for one another. That's what dad said, I just want to be with my mom because I miss her and need her."

Mrs. Dumpling said, "I am here now, and your dad will be coming back soon. Mr. Grant said that he has messengers and guards out looking for him. Benji, could you get some ice for Randy's ankle, I'll need some for his arm also. I have something here for you to take for pain Randy."

Daniel had returned to the room to notify Wilford that everything was ready. Wilford excused himself and left the room. Benji excused himself from the room for just a moment to ask Wilford and Daniel what was going on,

"Why does Mr. Grant have to go to the palace?"

Daniel replied, "John took a message to the Estate Guard hours ago and has not returned and there is no report been made to pick up the Teetsons."

Wilford abruptly said, "We must go."

Benji returned to the room and asked, Kathryn if she was hungry?

Kathryn replied, "Yes to tell you the truth."

Randy said, "He makes fantastic pancakes."

Kathryn looked at Benji and asked, "Are they Mr. Grants' mom's pancakes?"

Benji said, "Of course! They're the best would you like some?"

Kathryn smiled, "Yes, thank you."

Randy said, "I would like some,"

Benji said, "I will make enough for all of us."

Mrs. Dumpling said, "Randy, can you tell me what happened since you and your dad arrived at the Island of Reconciliation?"

Randy replied, "We got to ride in a carriage to take a ride of faith. The man gave us two black horses and when we opened our eyes we were on a bridge and the horses were white as snow. Dad had to do an act of kindness. What is that?

His mom said, "It's doing something nice for someone, or it can be for a lot of people, not just one.

Randy said, "Oh, ok. I started to have memories of an Uncle who had two sons, and they were always picking on me calling me Rainey, not Randy. Dad said he was going to drop me off at Uncle Terry's, and I asked him to just let me come with him, but he said, no, he had to take care of a personal matter for a friend. What's a personal matter mean mom?"

His mom said, "It could be something private that's only between two people,"

Randy said, "Like a secret?"

Mom replied, "Yes it could be. What happened at your Uncle Terry's cottage?"

Randy said, "Uncle Terry is mean! Where's Mr. Grant at? I told him everything can't he just tell you?"

"Well, I spoke with Mr. Grant, and he said it would be better for you to tell me because it would help you by telling someone whom you trusted that wouldn't hurt you."

"Mr. Grant didn't hurt me, he protected me, he's nice!"

His mom looked at her son and said, "He is very nice and always has been. There isn't anyone here who is going to hurt you and I won't let Uncle Terry, or his sons, Terry, and Steven, hurt you either. Randy, just take your time and let me know what happened so your Dad and I can decide how to handle it, ok?"

Randy said, "OK! When I got out of the carriage, they started picking on me calling me Rainey, I said my name is

Randy, they said ok Rainey, then when I went into the house with them, they grabbed my backpack and wouldn't give it back.

"Dad had a talk with Uncle Terry about not bullying me. Uncle Terry came in and told them to stop it! I finally got my backpack back. Then Uncle Terry took me upstairs to show me where I was going to sleep, he wanted me to sleep on a wet mattress. I told him that I knew that dad had talked to him about me not being bullied and that Terry and Steven would bully me all night and asked if he had another room.

"He pushed me into the closet and told me that was my room and locked the door. I couldn't get out." Randy started crying. "He wouldn't let me out, and they were all laughing about it in the hallway. I pounded on the door to let me out!

"My backpack was in Terry and Stevens's room, and I wanted it. When the door opened, I ran out to get it, Uncle Terry hurt my arm then. He said that dad wouldn't be back for a few days and went to get my new mommy and I told him I have a mommy and I love her." Tears were falling from his eyes as his mom held him while he was talking. "Terry and Steven ran off leaving me laughing about it, I fell down stepping in a hole outside. They're mean! I don't ever want to go back there. I prayed for Jesus to help me, and he did protect me here with Mr. Grant, Benji, and Phillip."

His mom was crying with her son as she held him, then told him, "Mr. Grant said he would take care of your Uncle Terry and his sons."

Randy said, "OK."

Benji came to get them to take them to the Great Hall to eat their meal. Randy looked up at the picture of Thaddeus Grant with Benji and Mr. Grant, he smiled as his mom carried him out of the room. As they left the picture changed to Randolph Grant with his arm around Randy, Benji standing by his side, and Thaddeus his mom Kathryn, and his dad Pastor Dumpling behind them.

Benji, while walking to the Great Hall, Jacob one of the messengers came to tell him that Mr. Dumpling would be arriving later as he had been found.

WOLF SHIELD

Mr. Grant returned to the Treasure Room where under the table was a secret lever that opened another door, behind the shield of Thaddeus Grant. Opening into another room he walked in, and the door closed behind him. He turned and looked at the door that had a message from Thaddeus Grant. The message was, "Grant is not your last name. Grant is who you are! You have walked through the door because you have decided to walk the path that has been chosen for you. You have decisions to make. First some questions. You must speak out loud your answer to each question before you will see the next question."

The first was written on the wall of the door. Your first question is from Alistair Grant
"Did you walk into the room with anger or concern?"

He said, "Both. Anger that someone could hurt a child and abuse him. Concern because a guard has not returned from a mission that he was given, and he is also a youngster who is growing into a man too quickly."

The first question disappeared and the second was written on the door.

Your second question is from Bennet Grant "Does the Anger outweigh the concern?"

"There is righteous anger and unrighteous anger, my anger is only because of hearing the actions of what has happened. My concern is what overrules the anger." The second question disappear and the third was written on the door.

Your last question is from Ranulf Grant "What would you do to correct each situation?

1. Terry Teetson and his two sons?"

"This is the Island of Reconciliation and I know exactly what I am going to do with him and his sons. I am going to let the Dumplings pray about it and let me know how they would like to handle it. I will be praying to seek the answer as well. Then the decision will be made."

2. Pastor Teetson who is now Pastor Dumpling?

"Regarding Pastor Dumpling who now is not the boy he was. I have no ill will against him, even if his name was still Teetson and was not a Pastor. Now he is my brother in Christ Jesus, so I will ask him to sit with me in fellowship to find out how he came about the name Dumpling?"

3. The Estate Guards who have your Manor Guard who are not being so kind to him, they have hurt him because he has not told them who you are.

"My intentions, for now, are to go see Thaddeus Grant who is the Grant of the Island of Reconciliation whom I will ask for his physician to take care of John my guard. Then I will ask him to pray with the son he never had who loves him. Then we will see how to handle the matter."

That was the end of the questions.

Ranulf Grant then informed him of the decisions he needed to make now. "You have two names. Jackson Randolph choose one name to go above your title as Grant of the Manor."

He answered "Randolph."

Ranulf informed him "The name Randolph means *Shield Wolf* and is the shield that is in the outer room agreeable?"

He answered "Yes."

"Your signet ring has your shield, and it is to be worn on your left index finger.

Choose your armor. For you will need it later."

He answered, "Silver for my guard, as for me, I have my armor that the Lord has provided for all that have been adopted through God's grace of salvation through his Son, Jesus. May I ask some questions?"

Ranulf replied, "Yes."

"How can the questions that have been asked be coming from the Grant of the past Ranulf, Bennet, and Alistair Grant's?"

Ranulf said, "You are on the Island of Reconciliation there are many things that you will learn now that you will be announced as the Grant. Things that you will need to correct and battles you will need to win to restore the Islands of Reconciliation."

Randolph Grant said, "You said Islands of Reconciliation I know only of one Island of Reconciliation."

Ranulf replied, "You have much to learn. Once you are in the Towers you will have much more understanding. Answering your question though, there are more islands and lands that are part of the Island of Reconciliation."

"May I have the wolf shield on the breastplate of the armor as well?"

Ranulf replied, "Yes. Thaddeus Grant awaits your arrival after you put your armor on. Pick up your sword which is the Word of God your Bible which also contains your clues for your adventures. Your swords of your guard also bear your shield of the Manor on its handle. You, also have a set of the armor you have for your guard should you need it. But! Your choice of Armor that you have shared with us is much greater."

Pastor Dumpling Comes Home

Pastor Teetson, on his journey to complete the act of kindness, wanted to hurry, so he could get back to his son. He traveled down the road and a red squirrel seemed to follow with him on his journey. He came to a road he remembered was a shortcut to his cousin's manor. When he began to turn on the road, the red squirrel had moved in the middle of the road and wouldn't move.

The Pastor backed the carriage up to go around on the left side. The squirrel was now there blocking his way. The Pastor smiled. Not wanting to take the chance on moving forward with the carriage and accidentally injuring the squirrel, he backed the carriage up again to go around on the right side when he turned around to look forward, the squirrel had moved to the right side.

So, he decided to back up and not go down the road but found it odd and strange that the squirrel was blocking his way. As he began his journey down the road again, he saw the squirrel following along.

He was now approaching Bennet Village where he had spent most of his time as a child bullying others. He turned on the main section of the village seeing a shop that was selling the

Grant Manor apples and remembered that he could have just gotten them out of the apple bins at the manor. Likewise, he pulled the carriage over tying the horses to the rail and went into the store to purchase some apples. He came out with a couple of bags for his journey. He heard a commotion across the street where a man was being harsh with an older couple. It reminded him of how he used to bully others as a child. Walking over he said, "Here now what is all the ruckus about? Why are you treating the elderly couple with such harsh words?"

The man looked at him and said, "It is no concern of yours be on your way!"

The Pastor replied, "Well I am making it my concern. What is the issue, and we will see if it can be rectified?"

The man looked at him and said, "Mind your own business and stay out of mine!"

The elderly lady began coughing and wasn't feeling very well at all. The Pastor turned to them and placed his hand on her and prayed, "Father in heaven please touch Mrs. and Mr. Clackson with your blessing in their time of need. I do not know what the issue is, and the man is being very harsh in his attitude towards them, I pray Father that you would soften his heart towards them in Jesus' name."

The Clacksons said, "Thank you for the prayers we can always use them."

The Pastor said, "Now tell me what the issue is?"

The man stared at them and said, "It is none of his business, and you will be quiet about it."

The Clacksons bowed their head in shame with fear to say anything.

The Pastor then turned to the man and firmly said, "You will not talk to them in this manner again! I have a check-in my spirit as to what this matter is about and if it is what I think is being done here then let your spirit hear what is to be said."

The Pastor then opened his Bible and proceeded to teach and preach. He said, "In the beginning, God formed man from the dust of the ground, and breathed into his nostrils the breath of life; and man became a living soul. And the Lord God planted a garden eastward in Eden; and there he put the man he had formed. And out of the ground made the LORD God to grow every tree that is pleasant to the sight, and good for food; the tree of life also in the midst of the garden, and the tree of knowledge of good and evil."

The man stood there with unbelief written all over his countenance. With a smirk of a grin and in an arrogant tone said, "Go on reading some more fairy tales."

The Pastor said to him "I will read more but this is no fairy tale and the spirit you serve knows it. And the LORD God commanded the man, saying, of every tree of the garden thou mayest freely eat: But of the tree of the knowledge of good and evil, thou shalt not eat of it; for the day that thou eatest thereof thou shalt surely die. And the LORD God said, it is not good that the man should be alone, I will make him an help meet for him. And the LORD God caused a deep sleep to fall upon Adam, and he slept: and he took one of his ribs and closed the flesh instead thereof; And the rib, which the LORD God had taken from man, made he a woman, and brought her to unto the man. Adam named her Eve, and she was his wife."

The Pastor then said, "The serpent showed up and deceived Eve by twisting what LORD God had said about the tree of knowledge of good and evil." As he spoke, those in the village were gathering around to listen.

The pastor said, "In the world where I have come from there are those whose light shines bright as servants of the Lord Jesus the Christ the Son of the Living God, and there are those that have reached out for the deceptive fruit from the evil one and who do his bidding of evil."

He turned, and he looked at the man and sad, "You were either born here on the Island of Reconciliation or you or your family were in the world before you came. If you were born here, then you were raised as I was with a hardened heart towards others and if you came from the world then you would have had to have repentance and faith to come to Harborshire and then to have a step of faith to come to the Island of Reconciliation. Again, I will ask, what is the issue that needs to be rectified?"

The man looked at him and said nothing.

The Clacksons said, "He is here to collect rent for the cottage we live in, and we have no money to pay the rent. He wants five coins for us and our three grandchildren who stay with us."

The Pastor said, "When did the Grant start sending others around to collect rent for living in the cottages? I don't recall when I lived here that there was ever any rent for living in the cottages."

Mr. Clackson's replied, "We don't know. This man showed up one day and said he was here to collect the rent we said we don't pay rent and his response was, 'you do now!'"

Pastor Teetson turned to the man and said, "Now I understand why you don't want them to say anything, and you probably have the entire village in fear, you are a thieving bully! I will find out if my judgment of you is correct and if it is not then I will apologize to you and then I will pay their rent of five coins. Now let me find out!"

As the Pastor walked to the podium in the center of the village. The man said, "What are you going to do?"

"I am going to find out."

He rang the bell for the villagers to come to gather around the podium. The man began walking briskly away for he knew he was in trouble. Pastor Teetson looked over and saw the red squirrel setting in a tree and seem to be watching him. The Pastor winked at the red squirrel.

As the villagers gathered around many asked, "Why is the bell ringing? Who is that at the podium and why did he ring the bell?"

The Pastor began to speak, "I am Pastor Dumpling, when I was younger, I lived in this village. I was mean and a bully. I am sure that I bullied a lot of you here today when you were children, and I was disrespectful to the older adults and the elderly.

"I met and married my wife here and we adopted a young boy. My wife and I had an argument and I behaved wrong towards her. She picked up our son and left. The next morning there was a knock on my door, and it was Thaddeus Grant's butler Benjamin. He said, 'Thaddeus Grant would like to see you,' and I went.

When I arrived at the Grant Castle Estates Community I was ushered to a cottage. Stepping in, my wife was there sitting in a rocking chair holding my son. Benjamin led me into another room where Thaddeus Grant and another gentleman named Wilford were located. Thaddeus Grant said some words to me that were a shock. He said, 'I am very disappointed in you.' I didn't even know he cared for me, a mean bully, that used to harass him and go on the estate property without an invitation trying to steal his delicious apples off the trees instead of going to the apple bins and asking for them. Then Thaddeus Grant said in a very firm tone 'Should you ever be mean to your wife as you were last night when she was brought to me by Wilford and if you ever cause any harm to the young precious boy that has been entrusted to you for care, then I will kick you and your entire family off of the Island of Reconciliation!'

He didn't stop there, he went on to say, 'Tell me, do you love the young girl you married? Because slapping her around isn't showing love. Do you love the boy? You don't like his given name? Tough! His name is not going to change. What are you going to do when he's older? You going to change his name for him when running around with your brothers Terry and Burt and their friends? You going to start calling him Rudy? Because if you love him and do that, you're going to lose him.' " Pastor Teetson continued speaking Thaddeus' words, "'Just like the other boy that used to live on the island when you and your cohorts started calling him that. His family moved away, and he was very dear to my heart. Tell me, how many friends do you have? Don't say I have a lot of friends that run with me, because they are not your friends. They run with you because they don't want to be a pawn in the games you play with other's lives.

Pride goes before a fall and your prideful arrogance with your belief that you are superior to everyone else doesn't surround you with friends. Your insolent with the adults and the elderly is rudeness and shows a lack of respect that they are due. You don't realize your actions towards others! I blame that on your Great Grandfather who was a billowing windbag of trouble.

Pastor Teetson continued, "'I am going to repeat this to you again, and you need to open your ears and heart to what I say, If you slap her again or mistreat her or the boy, I am going to kick you and your entire family off the island! Your wife is a very kind and loving person and there are those on the Island of Reconciliation who love and care for her. She and your son don't deserve to be treated with a lack of respect that you have shown, and I won't have it.'

"When he was done having his say. I stood there in my arrogant pride with my smirk grin and said to him our house isn't on the Grant Castle Estates Community grounds. Standing there like I was something! He brought me to my humble knees with what he said and did next.

"Thaddeus Grant said, 'I own the ground your house sits on, and I own the house that sits on the ground, and I allow for your family to stay in the house for free and the food provided to your family is freely given as to all on the Island of Reconciliation. Alistair Grant left all the lands and care to me for the Island of Reconciliation.' I was stunned! Why would he do that if I am such a disgrace to him and those on the island? I had a tear dripping from my eyes because I knew deep down for the first time in my life someone was showing tough love, but it was true love and care for me."

Continuing with the words of Thaddeus, Pastor Teetson spoke, "'Because the boy who moved away, whom you, your brothers, and all your cohorts emotionally abused, asked me to be kind to Kathryn's family that you are a part of now.' My jealousy began to rise because of this boy and Kathryn, and I said why would he do that? He said, 'because Kathryn was his friend, she was nice and deserved a blessing for her kindness to me.'

"She always treated me as she treated others on the Island with no hidden agenda.

He said to me, 'I have shown patience to you and waited for you to grow up, to realize that you have so much potential for doing good. I care for you and everyone here and even today you may not realize because I have had to show you a tough love of truth about yourself.

"You have a heart that is hardened, and you need to hear the truth. Letting your heart be convicted and softening and to repent of your actions, so you can accept the greatest and most valuable gift that is freely given which is salvation through the Lord Jesus the Christ the Son of the Living God. When you accept and receive Jesus into your heart your life is going to change. Albert you, your wife, and child will live in this cottage, not your brothers, or your cohorts, or any of your relatives, It's time for you to feed on the truth of the Word and not the lies of the world that you have had a steady diet of.

"This gentleman's name is Wilford; he is my aide and a man of god. He will visit with you once a week, here is a Bible, it is up to you whether you open it and read it and if you have any questions, you can ask Wilford, he will search the Written Word with you to find your answers.'

"Thaddeus informed me that I and my wife would now be known as Mr. And Mrs. Dumpling and that the boy's name would remain Randy, and if I called him anything other than his name, Thaddeus Grant said 'I will have Benjamin find me the biggest switch and I will turn you over my knee and give you the spanking you have never had.' I just looked at him as he and all of them left the cottage and I turned looking at my wife; she was smiling. Then she said, 'Hello Mr. Dumpling.' Little Randy pointed and said, 'Daddy Dumping!' I laughed. Within time, I accepted the free gift of Salvation that only comes through the Lord Jesus the Christ the Son of the Living God. My name use to be Albert Teetson and I am humbly asking if you would forgive my trespasses against you. I am deeply sorry for the way I treated you all."

Mr. and Mr.'s Clackson stood up and said, "We knew Albert Teetson, but now we see Pastor Dumpling. Welcome to the Bennet Village." Everyone in the village began welcoming Pastor Dumpling too.

Pastor Dumpling said, "I have one more question. Who is paying the man over there rent for living in your cottages, stores, shops? Everyone raised their hands"

He stared over at the man and asked, "Those in the village, why has no one gone to the Grant and told him?"

One of them said, "Because he and his men will not let us pass."

Pastor Dumpling said, "Who would like to ride in my carriage with me to tell the Grant?"

They were still afraid. No one said they would go. The man yelled from across the way with a laugh, "The rent is due by sunup tomorrow morning. Take your fairy tales elsewhere."

"There is a battle going on in the Bennet Village, and it is not a battle of flesh against flesh. It is a spiritual battle. Those of you who the Lord Jesus is your savior. It is written: For the LORD, your God is he that goeth with you, to fight for you against your enemies, to save you. It is also written: He will cover you with his feathers. He will shelter you with his wings. His faithful promises are your armor and protection. You only need to let your FAITH ARISE and go to him in PRAISE and PRAYER asking for His help and He will help!"

Silence went across the village and messengers who had been sent out to find Pastor Teetson began to sing praise in heavenly voices. "Sing, Sing, sing praises unto the LORD God, let your faith arise, praise the Lord, praise the Lord, go to him in prayer, He will cover you with his feathers, and shelter you with his wings. He is your refuge, praise the Lord."

The villagers began to sing praises unto the Lord and peace that passes all understanding began to fill their hearts with joy. The Pastor asked Mr. and Mrs. Clackson if they would like to ride with him, and they agreed. By the time he was done the day had turned to nighttime. They got in the Carriage as he turned to go back down the main section of the road, he looked at the tree and the red squirrel was gone. As they turned to go down Grant Castle Estate Blvd coming towards them were the red squirrel, the Grant Manor guards, and the messenger Michael.

Mr. and Mrs. Dumpling Reunite

Michael said, "Pastor Teetson we have been trying to find you to let you know that your Son Randy is at the Grant Manor, he is safe and being cared for. When you are done with your act of kindness you may come and pick your son up there."

Pastor Dumpling asked, "Why is he at the Grant Manor? I left him with my brother Terry did he do something to my boy?"

Michael said, "It would be best when you complete your act of kindness to speak with Mr. Grant at the Grant Manor. Your son has been watched over and is in safe care and protected."

The pastor replied, "I didn't know whether to leave my son with my brother and I prayed God would watch over and protect him."

Michael said, "God answered your prayer as well as Randy's."

Mr. and Mrs. Clackson said, "There must be a mistake here, there is no Pastor Teetson here." They looked at the Pastor and said "Only Pastor Dumpling. He has done more than one act of kindness today."

William the guard said, "Could you share with us the acts of kindness?"

Mr. Clackson said, "He has reconciled with the village for the time when he was a young boy living here. The entire village has forgiven him. He stood up to a man name Agar who has for many months had us pay rent for the cottages, stores, and shops that were provided to us for free by Thaddeus Grant. He was bringing us to see the Grant to tell him of this because Agar has his men block the road, so we cannot."

William said, "Where is this man?"

Mrs. Clackson said, "Silas can you show them and thank you for bringing the guard."

The red squirrel stood up and looked at William and showed him where Agar and all his men were.

Mrs. Clackson asked the messenger if he could take a message to Silas to let him know that there are some nuts on the porch for him.

Michael smiled and said, "He knows already. He is a smart squirrel. Come, I will take you to the Grant Manor and there is a doctor there who will help you Mr. And Mrs. Clackson."

Pastor Dumpling's mind drifted back to when he left the Island of Reconciliation. When he left years ago with his wife and son was because after becoming a Pastor while living at the cottage that Thaddeus Grant had provided for him and his wife and child to learn the truth and not to continue to live in the deception of lies that he had been brought up on. Thaddeus Grant offered him a flock who had just lost their Pastor who had passed on to be with the Lord. The church was in Bennet Village.

Fearing ridicule because his name now was Dumpling, not Teetson, he became upset within himself and bit into the deceptive fruit that was lying to him, instead of taking a step in faith. So, he left the island and ventured into the world. When he was in the world, he randomly opened his Bible and the following verse of scripture jumped out at him: *For I know the plans I have for you, declares the LORD, plans to prosper you and not to harm you, plans to give you hope and a future.*

Later that day while walking in the world, which was so different from the Island of Reconciliation, he heard a man on the street preaching and the verse of scripture he heard was: *And we know that all things work together for good to them that love God, to them who are the called according to his purpose.* Pastor Dumpling smiled. He had hoped that whoever the Grant was now that he would allow him to come home to Bennet Village to be their Pastor. Arriving at the Grant Manor he was greeted by Benji, Pastor Dumpling immediately recognized him as someone else he had bullied as a child.

Pastor Dumpling said, "I owe you an apology from when I was younger and picked on you. I am greatly sorry and hope you would forgive me."

Benji, replied with a smile, "Are you hungry? We're having Randolph Grant's mum's pancakes. They're the best with bacon, ham, and eggs."

Pastor Dumpling said, "Yes, but do you forgive me?"

Benji replied, "You're not the one who picked on me, it was your brother Terry and his cohorts, if you need forgiveness from me then I forgive you! Come let's go to the Great Hall to eat, drink milk, and be merry with reconciliation and joy. Your son Randy has never been in a Great Hall. When his mom was carrying him, he said it's the biggest dining room he has ever seen!"

Pastor Dumpling said, "Kathryn is here?"

Benji replied, "Yes, they are waiting for you."

As they walked into the Great Hall, Randy with a loud voice said, "Hi dad! I love you! Uncle Terry is mean!"

Kathryn got up and ran to her husband and gave him a big hug. She kissed him and said, "I love you."

Pastor Dumpling began crying for joy as God answered his prayer to be reunited in love with his Kathryn.

Pastor Dumpling said, "Randy, I am just so glad that you were protected, and I'm so sorry you were hurt." He fell to his knees crying. "Kathryn, why did you leave?"

Dr. Dumpling said, "I didn't leave, it's not your fault or my fault. When we have time, we'll talk about the other later."

"Dad, I got an answer to my prayer when you asked me to pray before getting left with Uncle Terry. You said God works in mysterious ways, so I prayed and asked God if he could do one of those mysterious ways for me because I didn't want to stay at Uncle Terry's house. Mr. Grant, Benji, and Phillip are my answer to my mysterious way prayer. Praise you JESUS! They protected me and kept me safe."

Benji said, "Randy, the messenger Michael, who found your dad, told me your dad wasn't sure about leaving you there and the only reason he did was because the family he was going to be with were much worse than your Uncle Terry and your cousins. Your dad also prayed that God would watch over and protect you. God answered your Dad's prayer for you too."

Randy looked at his dad and said, "God is wonderful, Praise you JESUS." He then put his hand on his dad's shoulder because he was sobbing with tears and said, "Dad, everything will be ok. I love you."

His dad said, "I love you too and your mom. Mrs. Dumpling you're going to have to get in line because I get the first crack at my brother Terry."

Randy said, "Mom and dad, wouldn't it just be better for God to take care of Uncle Terry? He might grow up one day and find his way to the Bridge of Reconciliation, the Cross of Christ Jesus."

Benji smiled and said, "Randy has been spending a lot of time talking with the Grant of the Manor."

Pastor Dumpling said, "I would like to meet him and thank him for watching over my son Randy. May I see him"?

"When he returns, I will let him know you would like an audience with him."

Pastor Dumpling said, "Thank you."

12

Journey To The Palace

Wilford, who was an aide to Thaddeus Grant asked,

"Randolph Grant. What were his intentions when he arrived at the palace to speak with Thaddeus Grant?"

Randolph Grant advised "The Estate Guard were notified to pick up Terry Teetson and his sons, and they didn't do it. Instead, the guard who was sent was mistreated and hurt by the Commander of the Estate Guard and is in their guardhouse. I will ask him to pray with me regarding how to handle the Teetsons."

Wilford replied, "And the guard?"

"The guard will meet Randolph Grant today" was the answer he gave Wilford,

Wilford said, "Then you are not going in anger?"

Randolph Grant replied, with a smile, "I was not happy with what has transpired. Anger is not an issue right now. My young guard and how the boy was treated on the Island of Reconciliation are my concern. The boy is very special. He heard his mom cry for him and his dad. How could that be if he has never been on the island before?"

Wilford replied, "He has been on the island before. Randy, and his adopted parents the Dumplings, lived here for a couple of years before they left to go into the world. A mother and daughter had arrived at Harborshire asking for me. Mr. Habens sent notice for me of their visit. Benjamin and I came to see who they were at Harborshire. I recognized the mother as she was a very old friend of mine, and I hadn't seen her in years when she had left Harborshire.

"Her daughter was a mirror image of her when she was her age. The daughter was holding a baby in her arms with love and care asking for me to find a good home for the child that would protect him. The daughter said his name is Randy and his name was never to be changed."

Randolph Grant said, "You thought Albert Teetson would be the family to place him with?"

Wilford replied, "I thought of Kathryn, whom you asked Thaddeus Grant to bless, along with her family, would be whom I would entrust with the child. I had no idea she would marry Albert. God works in mysterious ways. I inquired of the young girl as to why the boy's name was never to be changed. She stated that the family who adopts him may want to change his name." Her reply was, 'then find another family for my boy. He is special for he has been named after a leader that I and my husband are very fond of. We both desired for his name to be after the boy who came to our community hurting from the same type of pain our entire village was hurting from and as a young boy of twelve began to put a stop to it.'

"She went on to say that her husband was one of ten boys that were his best friends and that one betrayed him. He disappeared and no one knows what happened to him. There have been four attempts on our son's life. My mom shared with us that you once rescued her by bringing her here to Harborshire for safety. I told her, 'I knew of a young girl who'd watch and protect her son never changing his name and when he was of age, she would tell him of your love for him.' Then they returned to the world."

Randolph Grant asked, "What were their names?"

Wilford replied, "Are you the boy that went missing from their lives?"

Randolph Grant asked again, "What were their names?"

Wilford replied, "The mother of the child was named Allison. Everyone called her Ally. The husband's name was Jackson, but he went by JT. Their last name was Townsley."

Randolph Grant said, "The boy will stay at the manor where he will be protected. I will talk with Albert and Kathryn when I return to the Manor." He then said, "Driver, stop the carriage." He got out of the carriage. As he walked, he saw a fox in a snare and was talking to the fox with a gentle voice. No one could hear what he was saying. He released the fox from the snare then held him with comfort whispering in his ear. He then let him go.

He then walked back to the second group of the ten guards that were traveling with him for his safety and told them, "Scour the woods for any animals that are in snares and tell them gently, 'The Grant of the Manor has returned, and you will not be hurt.' Finally, release them from the snares. He then returned to the carriage to continue their journey.

Wilford asked, "Was that wise? Sending half of your guard away that was here to protect your journey to the palace so they can free animals that are snared?"

Randolph Grant replied, "This is the Island of Reconciliation. Why would I need guards to protect me? When I was younger living here on the Island of Reconciliation, I made friends with a lot of the animals. When I spoke to them, they could not understand what I was saying to them no more than I could understand when they made their noises to me to communicate. Yet, we had a bond of friendship that I would not hurt them, and they would not hurt me. The Lord provides for the sparrows and all animals for what they need, and will he not provide more for us who are his. I do not like snares, nor do I like traps that we may very well see on this journey to the palace."

Wilford then said with concern, "If, you feel there is going to be a snare or trap on our journey then why would you have sent half your guard away?"

Randolph Grant shut his eyes and smiled and said nothing.

"Wilford, let me know when you see Silas, I would like to see my friend."

Wilford stared at him giggling with astonishment. *He is a squirrel!* "We are on a trip to the palace, and you want to stop and see animals?"

Randolph Grant replied, "He is a smart squirrel." He smiled again and shut his eyes and said, "Let me pray now."

Time had passed while on their journey with no sighting of Silas. The outrider guards that were sent ahead to make sure the path was clear were approaching the carriage.

Wilford said, "Randolph Grant your outrider guards are coming."

He opened his eyes watching as one of the guards who were riding in the front of his carriage went ahead to meet them to see what the matter was.

His guard came back to inform Randolph Grant that the path was blocked by a fallen tree and when they would try to remove the blockage a red squirrel was running up and down the tree going crazy nuts.

Randolph Grant looked at them chuckling and smiling then said, "Send me my outrider guards." The guard motioned for them to come to the carriage as he went back to the front of the carriage. Randolph Grant recognized the young guards that were approaching once they were by the carriage; he asked them, "Did either of you ask the red squirrel which way he wanted you to go?" He just smiled at them waiting for an answer.

Alan, the youngest one, said, "After becoming frustrated with it, I asked: 'I guess you want us to go in a different direction?'"

"What did the squirrel do?"

"He sat down and shook his head yes!"

Randolph Grant tried to hold his laughing but to no avail and Wilford began laughing as well. Randolph Grant told his guards "The name of the red squirrel is Silas and that he has a knack for letting others know if there is danger going in certain directions and then gives a safer route to go."

He said to Alan and the other guard that was riding with him "Go back and tell Silas that the Grant of the Manor has returned, and you will not be hurt. Then say to come with you, then bring him to me."

The guards returned with Silas leading the way. When he saw who the Grant of the Manor was, he leaped into the arms of Randolph Grant.

Silas said to him, "How are you my old friend I've missed you." Then he hugged Randolph Grant and lay there on his shoulder.

Randolph Grant said, "I have something for you." and he gave him a nut. It was a special one that had been given to him by Ranulf for Silas.

Silas cracked it open and there was a message inside for him that only he could hear "Show Randolph Grant the quickest and safest route to the palace. Find Michael the messenger he will know why you have come to him. Now enjoy your treat."

Silas enjoyed his treat then jumped from the carriage, showed the quickest and safest route, then went to find Michael.

Randolph Grant was notified by the rearguard that the ten guards he had scoured the woods for the animals in snares and traps had returned. They continued their journey to the palace. Silas had found Michael, and he smiled giving Silas a stash of nuts and other treats that he carried back to his nest.

Michael sent out the call for the messengers and an eagle landed by Michael. Michael then gave him a key that Alistair had given to him; to give to the eagle who knew what to do with the key. As Randolph Grant, Wilford, the guards who were riding with them on the route that Silas had shown them arrived, they could see why his friend Silas didn't want them to go the route of the fallen tree. The Estate Guards were lying in wait for an ambush. Wilford then recalled what Randolph Grant had said about snares and traps on their journey.

After a while, the palace guard met them to lead them safely to the palace.

13

Assassination Attempt Foil

The palace Guard was leading the way to the palace. As they approached the palace that Randolph Grant hadn't been to or seen since his secretive arrival years ago. That was the time when Thaddeus Grant provided the Grant Manor for him to stay. As he approached the palace, he admired its massive size and its splendor of beauty with towers, turrets, and arch shaped windows. But something was awry within in his spirit. There was a check, but he didn't know what it was. Only in time would it become clear. It was troubling to him, and he prayed to God asking if He was trying to reveal something to him or was it just him?

Randolph Grant and Wilford got out of the carriage and were greeted by Benjamin, the aid to Thaddeus Grant. He advised that they had received word of their arrival from a messenger that Michael had sent. They were also advised of the situation as to why they were there.

Benjamin led them down the great hall to a private meeting room where Thaddeus Grant and another person were waiting.

Randolph Grant had not recognized the other one. He introduced himself as Malafide.

Randolph Grant began to ask Malafide questions "Where are you from?"

He responded, "I was born on reconciliation island."

"Did Thaddeus Grant give you that name? I only ask because he usually provides new names for those who live within the Grant Castle Estates community."

He responded, "I don't live in the community. I have a community garden further down the road from the Bennet Village. With the grapes on my vines, I make delicious wines."

Randolph Grant decided to stay silent to see if he would volunteer any more information because he knew what his name meant and everyone who was on the Island of Reconciliation had meaning associated with their names.

Malafide said, "I've brought a wonderful new wine today. It is hot. May I serve all of you some?"

"How did you come to meet Thaddeus Grant?"

He looked back at Randolph Grant and replied, "You have asked a lot of questions about me today, and it almost sounds as though you are suspicious of me for some reason, but we have never met before. Have I offended or wronged you in some way to be treated like this?"

Thaddeus Grant, Benjamin, and Wilford all remained silent without interfering.

Randolph Grant responded very firmly with, "I will ask you once again how you came about meeting Thaddeus Grant?"

He replied, "Well if it is that important to you to know, my nephew introduced me to him."

"Who is your nephew?"

Malafide looked at Thaddeus Grant to see if he would put a stop to all the questioning of him.

Thaddeus Grant looked back at him and said, "There is a red squirrel who always alerts others of danger when someone tries to go down a path they shouldn't, and he redirects them to a safer path."

Malafide said, "Meaning?"

Thaddeus Grant replied, "Well, I am curious where my son Randolph Grant is going with this. He too has a knack for these things, and he has caught my curiosity. Why are you so concerned with telling him who your nephew is?"

Randolph Grant turned to Benjamin and asked, "Why are you not serving the wine? You are Thaddeus Grant's butler are you not? Or have you been demoted?"

Benjamin replied, "I have been away and just returned today with good news for you. I am interested to see where we are going with this as well, how about you Wilford?"

Wilford responded with a giggle and said, "Randolph Grant has amazed me with our journey to the palace today, so yes, I am interested in how this is all going to tie together as well."

They all four turned and looked at Malafide, who was speechless and not saying anything.

Benjamin looked at the serving tray and saw there were four cups on the tray and asked Thaddeus Grant, "Sir, did you by any chance tell the wine man here how many would be meeting you in the room?"

Thaddeus Grant replied, "No. Why?"

"I was wondering how he would know to have four cups of wine on the tray ready to serve!"

Thaddeus Grant looked at him and said, "You didn't pour yourself a cup. Go ahead help yourself to a cup of your delicious wine." Thaddeus Grant turned to Randolph Grant and said, "His nephew is the commander of The Estate Guards."

Randolph Grant then asked, "Is this the same commander that has my young guard in his guardhouse? Who has mistreated him and hurt him? Is this the same commander who lay a trap of ambush for us on the way to the palace?"

Thaddeus Grant said, "WHAT?"

Wilford said, "It is true the Estate Guards were lying in wait for an ambush. Silas warned of the danger and showed us a quicker and safer route to the palace."

Randolph Grant said, "His name means intent to deceive."

Thaddeus Grant called for the palace Guard to take him and the wine away and commanded that no one drink the wine. "Get rid of it!"

Benjamin, Wilford, and Thaddeus Grant asked, "How did you know?"

Randolph Grant replied, "How much do they know?"

Thaddeus Grant replied, "They have been with me from the beginning Randolph, Benjamin has been my butler and bodyguard. They smiled "I couldn't make out Ranulf writing, and Wilford could. They are my trusted circle."

Randolph said, "Alistair told me that he had been poisoned and was given a message by a written note that the one who would succeed him would be poisoned also before the fifth grant was announced. Ranulf gave me a nut for Silas, and Bennet said he would have something here for me. We must pray. Terry Teetson and his sons have hurt and abused a child! He is Kathryn and Albert's son, and I have grown fond of the boy. They are at the Grant Manor.

Thaddeus Grant said, "We know a messenger arrived to let us know everything. I will deal with the commander of the Estate Guard!"

"Thaddeus, they mistreated and hurt one of my guards who would not reveal to them who I was. No! He is mine and his guard,"

Benjamin said, "We have notified the palace guards to pick up the Teetsons."

Wilford said, "Let us pray for wisdom!"

THE GATEHOUSE OF GIDEON
TRUMPETS BLOW

The eagle flew high to the castle's mountains that could only be reached by an eagle of the Grants. He flew with the key that would unlock The Gatehouse of Gideon for the trumpets to be blown. Randolph Grant had whispered into the ear of Daniel, his commander of the Manor Guards, when he left for the palace.

"Be of good cheer and rest easy with knowing that John will return. He has been injured. He will return with me when I come back to the Grant Manor. Now Daniel, when William and James return, place them as guards to the boy Randy for he is special. Wherever he goes they must follow. Let his parents know what I have instructed of you to do with the guards for their son. When I return, I will explain to them and tell Pastor Dumpling there are no ill will towards him. We will fellowship when I return.

"When you hear the heavenly voices sing then have the guard and those in the Manor pray for the Island of Reconciliation for I will be announced as Randolph Grant, then I will stand on the battlefield one against a thousand, so it will seem to those who stand against Thaddeus Grant and me, but we stand with one greater than we who are just mere servants of our Lord Jesus, the Christ the Son of the Living God.

"When you hear within your spirit the trumpets blow, do not fear for the armies of Grant Castle will stand on the mountains in all provinces of the Island of Reconciliation."

Daniel replied, "Yes sir."

The eagle flew high soaring across the sky drawing closer to the castle's mountains. He could see the Gatehouse of Gideon that would unlock the armies of each Grant's Castle where their armies of battle resided.

The Ranulf Castle that was in the Forest of Battleton was not one of these. The Ranulf Castle stood abandoned in the forest of Battleton that had been abandoned long ago.

The eagle landed at the Gatehouse of Gideon giving the key to the messenger who blew the trumpets to unlock the Castles of the Grants. Ranulf Grant led his army out riding on white horses with the banner colors of black and gold, their shields had an 'R' with a crown atop, a wolf on each side of the 'R.' Bennet Grant led his army out riding on white horses with the banner colors of silver and blue. Their shields had a cross engraved on them. Alistair Grant led his army out riding on white horses with the banner colors of blue and gold. Their shields had a cross with 'Defender of Man Kind' engraved on the shields. These were the three grants that had passed on and were those who had been entrusted with the care of the Island of Reconciliation.

Randolph Grant Is Announced

Wilford, Benjamin, Randolph Grant, and Thaddeus knelt praying for guidance and wisdom with the matter that stood before them. Wilford was the first to stand. Benjamin followed and then Thaddeus Grant. Randolph Grant remained praying.

Thaddeus Grant was informed that the Teetson boys had been pickup and were in a secure place and he handed Thaddeus Grant a book that one of them was reading. It was written by Jackson Randolph, and he wondered where he would have gotten the book.

Thaddeus Grant called for his commander of the palace guard and informed him to have the commander of The Estate Guard to have him, his officers, and all of his guards separated in groups of fifty, in twenty rows, and have them stand until the Grant comes out.

Randolph Grant opened his eyes, looked up, and saw Michael his messenger standing in the room with him.

Michael said, "Be of good cheer for today you will be announced as the Grant of the manor. You will be informed when leaving the room that Terry Teetson and three others have climbed over the south boundary wall here at the palace. They are all intoxicated save one of them. They currently are in the fruit trees as well. Three boys who watch the trees saw them and removed the ladders they used to get in the trees.

There are many within the estate guards who do not follow their Commander, there are those with hearts that are softened and confused, and there are those whose hearts have hardened that need to be softened. There are those whose hearts will not change."

Randolph Grant asked, "Michael, can you send a messenger to my manor to have Daniel my commander of the guard bring Benji and Pastor Dumpling here today quickly? I will need them here for what needs to be done."

Michael replied, "They are all on their way already and will be here within the hour. Thaddeus in his prayers asked for them to be brought here for he knew you would need them." Michael then left.

Wilford had the trumpeters sent to the top of the towers, The messengers were sent all across the Island of Reconciliation to announce the Grant that would preside at the Grant Manor and their heavenly voices began to sing.

Randolph Grant came out of the room looking around asked, "Benjamin where is Michael?"

Benjamin said, "I don't know, do you need for me to send a messenger for him?"

Randolph Grant replied, "Did he not just come out of the room?"

Benjamin smiled saying," No. I am here to let you know that the Terry Teetson and three others have been located."

Before he could say where, Randolph Grant said, "In the fruit trees."

Benjamin said, "Michael must have told you huh?"

Randolph Grant replied, with a nod.

"Benjamin has Sir Walter, Sir Issac, and Sir Robert ate yet?"

Benjamin replied, "Yes, would you like to see your friends?"

Randolph replied, "Yes I would, who are the three boys watching the trees and our guests?"

Benjamin replied, "they are the grandchildren of the Clacksons who live in the Bennet Village. The older boy Michael walked all the way from the village to see if he and his two brothers could work at the palace.? Thaddeus Grant brought the other two brothers to help Michael watch the fruit trees, the other brothers are much younger they are Daniel and John.

Thaddeus Grant came into the room to let Randolph Grant know the Estate Guards and Commander were his to handle when he was ready. "Oh, also Bennet Grant sent your Armor and Sword."

Randolph Grant said, "I have no need of the armor, I have my armor on already." He looked at the sword that was of the manor, then turned to Benjamin saying, "would you please give it to Benji to hand me that sword when I am ready."

Benjamin, "replied he's not here."

Randolph Grant replied, "he will be here within the hour with others."

Randolph Grant asks, "Thaddeus Grant when Pastor Dumpling arrives would you please send him to the field where the estate guards are telling him the Grant of the Manor from which he just came from ask him to preach to his captive audience until I arrive?"

Thaddeus Grant smiled replying, "yes! Thaddeus Grant asked, where will you be?"

"I am going to go see my old friends Sir Walter, Sir Issac, and Sir Robert, then when Benji arrives, I will take two of my guards with us to the fruit trees to bring Pastor Dumpling some more converts.

But first I will be going to get my guard John out of their guardhouse as Jackson Randolph and if any of them stand in my way then I will move them out of my way!"

Jackson Randolph left the room to go get John. As he walked through the guards to their guardhouse not one of them moved towards him for, they saw thousands upon thousands of guards standing on the field in front of them.

Many knew who he was, and they had already begun to be convicted by the softening of their hearts because he stood up for many of them when he lived here before. They had no idea though he would be the one standing on the field before them as the Grant of the Manor.

He carried John his guard out who was badly injured, and he stopped at the Commander of the Estate Guard and said to him, "I will see you later!"

John his guard said, "Jackson Randolph my friend forgives him for he knows not what he does, he is just a vapor in the wind that will pass, let the anger you have in your heart for him go." Then John turned to the Commander and said, "I forgive you."

Jackson Randolph carried his friend with tears flowing from his eyes to the physician who was waiting for them. As Jackson Randolph left the field he was announced as Randolph Grant.

16

RANDY MEETS HIS FAVORITE AUTHOR

Daniel the Commander of the Randolph Grant Manor had arrived with Pastor Dumpling, Kathryn, Randy, and Benji. Thaddeus Grant motioned to Pastor Dumpling to come to him, and he explained that Randolph Grant has asked you to go on the field and preach until he returns. Thaddeus explains the situation to him and also lets him know who Randolph Grant was.

Thaddeus Grant welcome Kathryn and Randy and told them, "Pastor Dumpling was called here to preach to a captive audience," and he smiled. He then called Benji and told him that Randolph Grant was on his way to see his old friends Sir Walter, Sir Issac, and Sir Robert and would like for him to join him.

Randy said, "Sir, where's Mr. Grant? Is he ok? He's nice and protected and took care of me."

Thaddeus Grant looked at Kathryn asking, "if it would be ok with her if he was to put Randy on his shoulders and walked him to see Mr. Grant before he takes care of a situation?"

Kathryn said, "that would be fine, but bring him back," and she smiled.

Benjamin walked Kathryn to the towers, so she could hear her husband preach.

Randy said, "You're the one in the picture with Mr. Grant and Benji."

Thaddeus replied, "Yes, but the picture has changed you'll need to go see it now when you go back to the manor."

Randolph Grant called for, Sir Walter, Sir Issac, and Sir Robert who were three bullmastiff dogs, and they came running and knock him down, jumping all around him as he smiled and said, "I guess you remembered me huh?" They all sat down in front of him, and he said, he was going to take them for a walk when Benji arrived.

Thaddeus Grant said, "I have a friend here who has been asking questions about you." Randolph Grant turned and saw Benji, and Randy was on Thaddeus Grant's shoulders. Thaddeus Grant set Randy down, and he stared at the big dogs.

Randolph Grant said, "They won't hurt you, come here, let me introduce you to them. This is Sir Walter, Sir Issac, and Sir Robert. Did you bring Phillip with you?"

William the guard said, "No sir.

Randy and I are going to go over here and have a talk. What do you think of the palace.

Randy said, "It's a bigger version of the manor."

Randolph Grant replied with a smile, "Yes, it is. I have to tell you something and I hope you won't think ill of me."

Randy said, "What's that mean?"

He replied, "Well it means I hope you won't be mad at me. Remember when you said that your favorite author was Jackson Randolph?"

Randy replied, "Yes, then said my cousins took my book that he wrote."

Thaddeus Grant said, "The Teetson boys had a book by your favorite author when we had them pick up, I have your book it's safe."

Randy said, "ok thank you."

Randolph Grant said, "Randy, I am Jackson Randolph, and I couldn't reveal that to you before because of a personal matter, so I hope you won't be mad at me?"

Randy said, "I know the book Benji gave me to read had a picture of you. Mom, and Benji it had all your names on the back of the picture.

"So, you're not mad at me?"

Randy said, "No, I love you."

Randolph Grant replied, "Well I love you too. Now though you're going to be hearing everyone call me Randolph Grant."

Randy looked at him and said, "I'll have mom explain that to me she's smart. Can I just call you Mr. Grant?"

Randolph Grant replied, "Yes you can. Listen I have to go, and I'll be back ok."

Randy replied, "ok."

Captive Audience

$\mathcal{P}$astor Dumpling walked out on the field recognizing many of the guards and the Commander of the Estate Guards, but they did not recognize him, some stared at him believing they had seen him before but could not recollect where or when it was.

Albert Teetson had not been on the Island of Reconciliation in years and when Thaddeus Grant sent Benjamin for him after his incident with Kathryn, Albert went with Benjamin he was never seen again on the island outside of Grant Castle Estate community.

Pastor Dumpling began speaking not revealing to them who he was, he said, "It is my understanding that I have a captive audience today" as he smiled then continued to speak introducing himself as Pastor Dumpling. "I've been asked by the Grant to come speak with you today before he returns to step on the field with you."

"It was brought to my attention that a boy was hurt and abused today, that word was sent to your commander to pick up those that caused the infliction, instead of doing what was asked of him, he decided to hurt and abused the youngster who was sent with the message."

"In the book of Matthew Chapter 7 verses 3-5 it is written: And why beholdest thou the mote that is in thy brother's eye, but considerest not the beam that is in thine own eye? Or how wilt thou say to thy brother, Let me pull out the mote out of thine eye; and behold, a beam is in thine own eye? Thou hypocrite, first cast out the beam out of thine own eye; and then shalt thou see clearly to cast out the mote out of thy brother's eye."

"My beam in my own eye got pulled out a long time ago, so I see very clearly to cast out the mote from your eye. I once was a bully, and I was fantastic at it! My heart was hardened towards others, I was in pain, a spiritual pain of emptiness, so I would lash out at others. I had many others who ran with me, they were not my friends, it was pointed out to me that they were my cohorts who fear that I would make them a pawn in the games that I unleashed on others."

"Many of you were in the group that ran with me. Oh, I see that has caught your attention. Tell me have you figured out who is standing before you today preaching if the answer is no then let me tell you. I am Albert Teetson."

"The morning that Benjamin came to my door he informed me that Thaddeus Grant wanted to see me. Thaddeus Grant was the conduit that God worked through to open my eyes to the truth of God's love for me and his love is there for you. I was blind but now I see. I was lost but I was found. I was walking in sin, and I was forgiven. My brother Terry Teetson was the one who abused the boy, and his sons are the ones who cause the boy to be hurt. My flesh wanted to get a hold of my brother and in a moment of time, the feelings that I had as Albert Teetson was upon me cause the boy, he abused was my son. Randy is a boy filled with kindness, joy, and has a heart for the Lord."

"I and his mother Kathryn we wanted to get our hands on Terry but out of the mouth of my son came these words 'Mom and dad, wouldn't it just be better for God to take care of Uncle Terry? He might grow up one day and find his way to the Bridge of Reconciliation, the Cross of Christ Jesus."

"My son today has spent the hours today with a Mr. Grant at the Grant Manor he was my son's answer to his prayer. I will say this to you, for all of you that I hurt when I was younger, I am sorry and can only hope one day you will forgive me as I hope Jackson Randolph will forgive me. This decision is not your commanders or your officers to make for you this is your own personal decision. Open your ears to hear the call that is calling you, let the hardness of your heart soften, repent of our sin, Jesus stands at the door, knock, and invite him into your heart, and your life will change and then be baptized, announce it to everyone that Jesus is your Lord and Savior."

He then knelt and prayed until the Grant returned to the field.

ome on Sir Walter, Sir Isaac, and Sir Robert as they came running," Randolph Grant said, "Good boys" as he and Benji were patting them and said, "Let's go."

"There are three boys out here who are watching the fruit trees and the guests sitting in them unable to get down because the boys removed the ladders they climb to get in the trees. The boys' names are Michael, Daniel, and John they are the grandsons of the Clackson's they will be returning with us. I am curious why they would leave them to come all the way to the palace to earn some payment when they could have found the same, I am sure at the Bennet Village."

Benji replied, "There was a man named Agar who was charging rent for everyone who was living in the cottages, stores, and shops. Pastor Dumpling saw where the man was being harsh with the Clacksons and found out that they were being charged five-coins rent for them and the grandson's so that is why they came to the palace."

"The man also had the road blocked so no one could come to tell you about it and his men would empty the Grant Manor apples that were to be given free in the tower bins for anyone who wanted some, they were selling them to the stores to resell and then taking all but 10% of what was being charged."

Pastor Dumpling reconciled with the Bennet Village and preached the Word of God to them as he stood on the center stage in the village.

"The Clacksons were coming to tell you about them riding in Pastor Dumplings carriage."

Pastor Dumpling said, "A red squirrel stopped me from taking a shortcut for the act of kindness I had to do and because I couldn't go the shortcut, I stayed on the road leading me to the Bennet Village."

Randolph Grant asked, "Did you tell him the name of the red squirrel as he was laughing."

Benji replied, "Yes, and about him. Randy wants to meet Silas and I told him that could be arranged. Randy is very special, and he loves you for protecting and caring for him."

Randolph Grant replied, "It was God who provided for him, and it is God to who all the glory belongs. I was just glad that God chose us to care for and protect him. I am sure that Randy loves you and Phillip as well."

Benji replied, "Ah yes, he has told us more than once and gave us each a hug. Why have you put the guards William and James as his guardians and protectors?"

Randolph Grant replied, "He is very special and one day it will be shown why." He knew but didn't want to say anymore even though he trusted Benji with the reason as to why.

Benji said, "Do we know who the guests are in the trees?"

Randolph Grant said, "There are four altogether, but I only know the name of one and that is Terry Teetson. I brought two of our guards with us Samuel and Severin hoping they might know who the other three are."

Randolph Grant turned around and motioned for the guards to come to him, he said, "How are you both doing?"

Samuel and Severin replied, "We are doing fine."

Randolph Grant asked, "Is it the first time that you have been to the palace?"

They replied, "Yes sir and it is a wonderful sight to see."

Randolph Grant said, "We are going to the fruit trees where there are four individuals sitting in the trees. One I know is Terry Teetson should you know who any of them are please let me and Benji know."

They replied, "Yes sir."

The dogs began barking when they saw the boys and one of the boys was on the ground holding his head from what they would learn from being hit with pears that had been thrown at them. They could see from a distance that two of them were climbing down the trees.

Randolph Grant said, "Sir Walter, Sir Isaac, and Sir Robert go boys and pointed to the two climbing down the trees."

Benji ran up to the boy that was hurt and asked, "Are you, ok laddie?" The boy was the smallest one named John, who was very shy and when he would talk, he had a stutter and wouldn't talk because others not his brothers would tease him and bully him because of it, and they found out Terry was one of them and his sons.

Benji told, the little boy that it is ok and that he once was a stutterer too and John looked at him with his eyes wide open. He was amazed because Benji didn't have a stutter when he talked.

John said, "How...ho..w...ho..w did you sto..p."

Benji said, "Do you like to sing?"

John nodded yes.

Benji said, "When you sing do you stutter then?"

John smiled and shook his head no.

Benji said, "Let me hear you sing."

John looked around with shyness and Michael and Daniel said, "He has a beautiful voice go ahead John, sing."

John began to sing and everyone smiled with joy listening to him sing unto the Lord, "Praise, Praise, Praise the Lord he watches over me and my family, I praise Him forevermore, oh Lord if it is in your will, I hope one day I'll be able to speak without stuttering, oh Lord, if it is not in your will, I'll still praise you forevermore, you are my Lord Jesus, I love you."

Benji, Randolph Grant, and the guards all had tearful joys falling from their eyes as they each wiped away their tears.

Benji said, "John, we have a doctor who can help you with the answer to your prayer, when I was little like you, a young girl helped me, and she is the doctor that I speak of. She is here with us at the palace and you, and your brothers will be going back with us to the Grant Manor and the Doctor, and her family will also. Your grandparents are at the Grant Manor."

Michael his brother said, "We can't go back until we earn enough to pay the rent of five coins."

Randolph Grant looked at Michael and said, "There is no rent due, and the man who took advantage of your family and those living in the Bennet Village I will deal with him when we are back at the manor."

Michael was the older of the three boys and said, "Sir may I ask who you are?"

He replied, "I am Randolph Grant, I am the Grant of the manor who has returned. There is no reason for you and your brothers to fear or worry about all that has happened it will be rectified."

The guards started laughing as everyone look the dogs were chasing those that climb down from the trees, they were all running around, the men were trying to get back up the trees, one made it up with ease the other lost his pants when he was climbing the tree, Sir Walter got a hold of them, and the man went up the tree without them.

Randolph Grant said, "Does anyone by any chance know which one that is?"

Severin said, "That is Burt Teetson he is a harmless soul, but his brother Terry picks on him quite a lot."

Randolph asked, "Do either of you recognize any of the others?"

Samuel said, "Burt is in the tree to the left, Terry is in the middle tree, the first tree to his right is Neville, and the one further to the right his name is Jonathan."

Randolph Grant stepped forward just staring at all of them.

Benji asked the boys, "Did they all throw the fruit at you?"

Daniel said, "Only Terry threw the fruit at us and shouted a lot of meanness towards us, and he would take care of us and our grandparents when he got us back to Bennet Village and that is when John said you leave them alone! Terry then started calling him names and throwing the fruit at him only, hitting him multiple times."

Randolph Grant listened to what was being said and then said, "There is a lot of fruit on the ground that needs to be picked up and put back in the trees."

Samuel the guard was smiling and asked, "Sir how are we going to get the fruit to stay in the tree once it's been pulled off its stem?"

Randolph Grant looked at Benji smiling and then said, "You got any ideas,"

Benji replied, "Well we could just try to throw it back at that middle tree where it all came from and see if any will stick to the tree."

Randolph Grant said, "Hmm, that is a great idea. Michael, Daniel, John, Samuel, and Severin come with me."

Benji said, "What I am to stay here don't I get to come too?"

"I thought you had a bad arm."

Benji said, "Not for throwing fruit at Terry I don't,"

"Well come on."

Randolph Grant said, "Everyone pick up all the fruit and I will be back in a minute, Hello Terry Teetson, so I hear you like to throw fruit at children, and you also like to threaten them and let us not forget about you grabbing a little boy's arm today and bruising it severally and you're other abused to him."

Terry, still drunk said, "Who are you?"

Randolph Grant said, "I am the Grant of the manor who has returned. We will be throwing the fruit back your way for each piece of fruit that drops to the ground that you do not catch you will walk back to my manor without your pants. Where you will be put in stocks and every child in the Bennet Village and surrounding areas will then spank you for being not so nice. After then the grown-ups will have their turn-taking a paddle to your behind, then you can relax while Pastor Dumpling reads the Bible to you, all of it. Commence throwing everyone."

Jonathan yelled from the tree he was sitting in "SIR, MAY I THROW SOME FRUIT AT HIM TOO?"

Randolph Grant walked over to the tree he was setting in and said, "Come down."

Jonathan climbed down from the tree.

Randolph Grant said, "Why would you want to throw fruit at the person you came with? Climbing over the boundary wall, climbing the ladder to get into the tree for some fruit?"

Jonathan replied, "I didn't come with them, sir. I came after Terry Teetson to give him a piece of my mind and to informed him to keep his brats away from my little girls Alba my five-year-old and Annabel who is seven because they have been teasing and bullying them to tears. When I would try to climb the ladder to his tree, he would throw the fruit at me. Then I heard someone yelling WHAT ARE YOU DOING IN THE PALACE FRUIT TREES! That's when I started to run for the wall to get over it. Hearing someone say one is running go for the guard I looked back and saw they were the boys, and they were taking the ladders away, that is when I climb the ladder. Wherever Terry was going I was going to have my say."

Samuel said, "Sir we have thrown all the fruit at Terry, and he doesn't catch very well."

Randolph Grant said, "Pick up all the fruit and give him another chance to catch some. John, did you hit him with any?"

John nodded no.

Randolph Grant replied, "Severin, you are taller than Samuel. Let John set on your shoulders while he throws the fruit at Terry. Daniel and Michael were you able to hit Terry with any?"

Michael said, "I hit him a few times sir,"

Daniel said, "Not yet sir when I throw at him, he keeps moving."

Randolph Grant, motioned to Jonathan stay where he is at and then said, "Terry would you like to come down out of the tree so everyone would have better aim at hitting you with the fruit or sit still while Daniel throws at you for a while by himself?"

Terry just looked at him and said, "WHAT?" Then he said, "Do you know who I am?"

Randolph Grant smiled and replied, "Do tell us who you are and then I will tell you what you are."

"I am Terry Teetson, and all of this island belongs to me and my family. Our birthright was stolen from us by Thaddeus. Alistair's last name wasn't Grant, it was Teetson and somehow Thaddeus let Alistair believe he was one of the Teetsons when he gave it all to him. When my Great, Great Grandfather, Horace Brackenshens tried to reclaim our birthright pleading for what was right that our family should be the ones who are the heirs, Thaddeus the old man ordered with meanness to have Horace knocked to the ground by Benjamin more than once in front of his family for humiliation. "

"So he went into the palace that belongs to us and Benjamin the bully threw him out and then Thaddeus told them he would kick them all off the island if they continued to spread a lie that wasn't a lie, or they could stay, and he would build two manors one for the Teetsons and the other for the Brackenshens but away from the village out in the woods. He still eventually kicked my Great, Great Grandfather and his family off the island and then kick us out of the Manors. That's who I am."

Randolph Grant said, "You have been lied to and it's time for you to learn the truth. The truth shall set you free from the anger that lies within you. Benji, go back with Michael to the palace return with the ledger of that time and lots of coffee to sober all of them up. Sir Isaac goes with Michael and Benji for protection. Oh Benji, come back on horses and bring a carriage with enough horses for the rest for I must get back to the field.

Benji, replied "I will return quickly."

Before they left Randolph Grant talked to Benji quietly where no one could hear and then they left. "Samuel, Severin, bring them all down from the trees except Terry he can stay where he is for now."

Terry began yelling meanness from the tree and Randolph Grant told him to be quiet or he would allow Jonathan to come up his tree. Terry shut up immediately for he was afraid of Jonathan.

Randolph Grant then said, "Rest your head on that branch and take a nap we'll wake you when everyone gets back." Soon he was asleep and snoring.

He then found out that Jonathan had taken up for Burt who Terry had been picking on, Burt invited Jonathan and his family to stay with him. Jonathan was a handyman.

Randolph Grant said, "they needed a handyman at the manor and he and his family would return with them, and he would provide a cottage for them."

Neville was downcast because his community farm had been taken away from him where he grew the best grapes. The community farm was just outside of Bennet Village which was the community farm that Malafide had spoken of. Neville had said someone from the palace had come telling him he no longer would have his community farm.

Randolph Grant asked, "what the name of the person from the palace was?

He couldn't recall but said he would recognize him if he saw him. Randolph Grant told him if his story checked out his farm would be returned to him.

He found out regarding Burt that he missed Albert, Kathryn, and little Randy, that Albert and especially Kathryn wouldn't allow Terry to pick on him. Randolph Grant informed him that he would see Albert again.

Benjamin, Michael, Sir Isaac, and the Manor Guards had arrived with all that Randolph Grant had asked for.

Benji returned with everything that Randolph Grant had

asked for. Randolph Grant had his guards sober up their guests. He also put Neville under protective guard. Burt was allowed to put his pants back on and Terry remain in the tree snoring.

Benji said, "Wilford wanted to come along, but I said no. I said it firmly."

Randolph Grant said, "Who and what else did he want?" He wondered all the way back why he would want to come; his duty was to be on the towers with the trumpeters.

"Severin would you wake up sleeping beauty up there and tell him to come down out of the tree. He is to sit over here on the log and bring Burt over here as well, so I can talk with them about the truth of his false claims." Severin did as he was asked and sat both Terry and Burt down on the log and both were brought some coffee and fruit to eat.

Randolph Grant advised Terry and Burt that he would be going over the truth with them because they have been lied to and the facts of what happened did not line up with what they have been told. "Terry, you said: 'I am Terry Teetson, and all of this island belongs to me and my family. Our birthright was stolen from us by Thaddeus. Alistair's last name wasn't Grant, it was Teetson and somehow Thaddeus let Alistair believe he was one of the Teetsons when he gave it all to him.' What I hold in my hand is the ledger of account of what transpired regarding everything that happened from Alistair giving the land to Thaddeus Grant your birthright was not stolen from you and the island does not belong to you and your family."

"It reads: 'I Alistair Grant whose last name is Castellan, but I go by Grant because that is who I am. I have watched over these past five years everyone on the island to find and select the person who would become the next Grant. Because of the will that Ranulf has left the Island of Reconciliation cannot be given to any of my family members or anyone on the staff. There are three that I have watched and have chosen Thaddeus Frost to give the care and protection of the island too. Thaddeus will become the new Grant. I write this on my bed dying. I have summoned for Thaddeus to come to my private chamber where I will meet this young boy for the first time, he has just turned fourteen, his love for God shows me that he is the correct choice.'"

"Terry and Burt, your birthright was not stolen, this island doesn't belong to you or your family, Alistair's last name was not Teetson, and Thaddeus Grant had not even had met Alistair to talk with him until the day he was selected to be the next Grant.

There are also five witnesses who have signed the ledger of this being truthful."

"You then said: 'When my Great, Great Grandfather, Horace Brackenshens tried to reclaim our birthright pleading for what was right that our family should be the ones who are the heirs, Thaddeus the old man ordered with meanness to have Horace knocked to the ground by Benjamin more than once in front of his family for humiliation.' We have already proven that your birthright was not stolen."

"The ledger reads regarding the incidents of that day with Horace Brackenshens and your family. 'The Teetsons and the Brackenshens who were distant cousins of Alistair Grant (by a note Alistair had written claiming such) came to the palace demanding that the island belongs to them for they were Alistair family, that they then began dictating what positions they would hold and that they would live in the palace. 1. They didn't live in the palace with Alistair Grant he had provided them cottages to live in, but it was never enough for them. 2. The island was not left to them, so it didn't belong to them. 3 Regarding that they were family and should be heirs. By the will of Ranulf that just could not be the case, the Island of Reconciliation could not be left to family or staff. 4. Thaddeus Grant was not an old man he was a young lad who was fourteen. 5. Thaddeus did not order Benjamin to knock down Horace Brackenshens to the ground for humiliation. Benjamin was selected by Thaddeus Grant to be his Butler and Bodyguard, Horace charged Thaddeus Grant, and his bodyguard Benjamin protected him by tossing Horace to the ground and telling him if he tried it again, he would land harder the next time.' There were five witnesses again to what was true in the ledger written of this incident. So he went into the palace that belongs to us and Benjamin bully threw him out and then Thaddeus told them he would kick them all off the island if they continued to spread a lie that wasn't a lie, or they could stay, and he would build two manors one for the Teetsons and the other for the Brackenshens but away from the village out in the woods. That's who I am."

"We have already proven that the palace did not belong to your family. The ledger reads that Horace Brackenshens stormed into the palace demanding with an arrogance that the palace and the Reconciliation Island were theirs. Benjamin grabbed him by the seat of the pants and tossed him out of the palace because he was not invited into the palace and was continuing to make accusations that were not true. "

"Thaddeus Grant praised and prayed for guidance, Benjamin laid down to sleep and Wilford fell asleep. In the morning Thaddeus Grant handed a scroll to Wilford and told Benjamin to have the guard take the two families down to the pier you and Wilford are to go with them, and Wilford is to read the scroll. They arrived at the pier. Wilford unrolled the scroll what Thaddeus Grant had written and asked Benjamin if he would like to read it. Benjamin said, "Thaddeus gave it to you to read. It read Horace Brackenshens is a Billowing Windbag of Trouble and I will not stand for his lies or his frivolous demands for his family and the Teetsons. The boat of faith will be arriving soon get on it and get off my island of course you'll have to have faith to ride the boat of faith, or you will be swimming to land other than the land you're standing on, or you can have a manor built for you in the Forest of Battleton, of course, you'll have to swim there as well. My guess is you would rather stay on my island? The deal is this I will build you a manor for the Brackenshens and Teetsons to live in away from the palace and the Village and there will be no more lies coming from your mouths, or you will be swimming. Now you can sit there until I figure out where to put your manor. The Teetsons asked for a separate manor from the Brackenshens, and Wilford said he would talk to Thaddeus Grant to see if that could be done. Benjamin said, 'I can tell you now the answer is no!' Thaddeus Grant built them a manor in the forest of Wary Mist. There were twelve witnesses to the truth of what was written here."

Randolph Grant finished with the last thing Terry had said, "That's who I am."

"So, we have established by the ledger Terry who you are not. Now, I am going to tell you who you are. You are a bully who is mean to everyone. You walked around with a puff out chest that I am important, bow down to me attitude, you bully your family, children, adults, elderly, and you bullied a child left to you by your brother Albert to care for his son, who told you and your sons not to bully him. You have raised two boys who are going to be just like you! This all comes about because you have been lied to apparently by those in your family, now if the lies that you have been told are not from your family then tell me who it is that has been lying to you and I will, or Thaddeus Grant will sit with them and tell them the truth, and then we will pray on what to do with them or that person. "

"There will be no more bullying by you or your sons to anyone on this island. You even bullied me when I live on this island when I was younger and your brother Burt too. I am Jackson Randolph who has been selected by Thaddeus Grant to

109

be the Grant of the Manor, I forgave you a long time ago, both of you, but what you did to Randy, Albert, and Kathryn's son when left in your care did not sit well with me."

Burt interrupted "Albert, Kathryn, and Randy are on the Island of Reconciliation? He turned to Terry and said why didn't you tell me? What did you do too little Randy? He then punched him in the side of the head and yelled at him DON'T YOU EVER HURT HIM AGAIN!"

Terry just looked at Burt and said, "It's about time you hit me, I've been waiting all these years to find out what it would take for you to hit me." He then looked at Randolph Grant and said, "So what are you going to do to me?"

Randolph Grant replied, "What do you think I should do to you?"

Terry replied, with tears in his eyes, "I don't know."

Randolph Grant said, "I am going to let Albert and Kathryn decide what should be done regarding how you treated Randy then they can tell me, I also will be praying regarding that situation, and I will be the one to make the decision. Randy has already said what he would like done."

Terry said very sheepishly, "What?"

Randolph Grant said, "He told his mom and Dad wouldn't it just be better to give Uncle Terry to God and let him handle Uncle Terry, he may grow up one day and walk on the bridge of reconciliation, the cross of Christ Jesus."

Terry sat there not making a sound.

Randolph Grant said, "You think about that while we travel back now to the palace."

Choose This Day

When Randolph Grant had returned from his visit with Terry Teetson and his friends who had climbed over the south boundary wall to visit the palace's fruit trees. He was greeted by Thaddeus Grant and Benjamin. They ask how his visit was with their guests at the fruit trees.

Randolph Grant said, "Very fruitfully."

Pastor Dumpling rose from praying turned and walked away bowing his head in prayer that their hearts were opened to hear what was said because they would choose this day. Randolph Grant looked and saw Randy in the tower above with Wilford and Kathryn he had a cheerful grin and was clapping his hands from hearing his dad preach.

Pastor Dumpling made his way to Thaddeus Grant, Benjamin, Benji, and Randolph Grant, he looked at Randolph Grant downcast for how he had treated him when they were younger, as he began to say something to him.

Randolph Grant said, "So, then did you soften them up for me? For I fear they will not like what I am about to say to them."

Pastor Dumpling replied, "I hope their hearts were open to the Word and the message."

Randolph Grant replied, "Benji shared with me what you did for the Clacksons and you're reconciling with the Bennet Village would you like to be their Pastor?"

Pastor Dumpling replied with cheerful tears, "Yes!"

"Would you also like to mentor a couple younger men as pastors for the villages "I will be building around the Grant Manor?"

Pastor Dumpling said, "Yes, I would, but why are you blessing me so much with the way I treated you when we were younger?"

Randolph Grant replied, "We all fall short of the glory of God, I have no ill will towards you, I forgave you long ago, I read a scripture verse that said in order for me to be forgiven, I must forgive as the Lord forgave. We will talk more, but first, it is time for me to have my say on this field."

Pastor Dumpling turned to Thaddeus Grant and said, "He forgave me."

With the tears still falling from his eyes Thaddeus Grant reached out pulling him closer with a fatherly hug telling him, "I told you he would! Now let's go to the tower and watch him spanked them but good."

He walked with confidence to the field with Benji by his side carrying the sword from the manor with him. As they made their way to the field that the Commander of the Estate Guards, his officers, and his guards had been standing, the trumpets on the towers began to blow, the heavenly voices of the messengers were still heard throughout the entire Island of Reconciliation. He was announced the Grant of the Manor has returned, Randolph Grant.

He looked across at all the guards and began to speak and all could hear him clearly. "I do not doubt that many of you who stand before me had nothing to do with what I am about to charge against you. After I speak if you did not participate in any of the events drop your sword and walk off the field with honor. Should you see any who did participate and are walking off with you point them out there is no dishonor in the truth for the truth shall set you free? Those that are pointed out will return to the field. Who I speak to today are those of you who have been involved in the treachery for those who are not involved listened for what is said to those who stand with you without honor."

"Today, a boy was abused and hurt on the Island of Reconciliation. I had my commander of the guard send a messenger who was a young guard with the message to pick up those that cause the abuse and hurt. Your Commander instead chose to mistreat, hurt, and put him in your GUARDHOUSE chained." He then motioned to Benji for the sword taking the sword he forcibly put it into the ground and said, "YOU will have an important decision to make here today!"

"I am the boy that used to live on the island that many of you would surround wanting to fight, and you would think it was a weakness when I would walk away while you all laugh. I stand here today to tell you it takes more courage to walk away from a fight that you cannot win rather than be beaten by a bunch of bullies. I have forgiveness in my heart my guard John a youngster of fifteen who I carried out of your guardhouse reminded me of. He has more courage than any of you who stand here before me today. His loyalty to me showed his courage when you would beat him to try to tell you who was living in the Grant Manor, was it so important that you would beat a child who is more man than any of you? "

"How many of you mistreated and beat my guard?"

"How many of you stood laughing over and taunting him?"

"How many of you took no thought for the boy who was abused and hurt?"

"How many of you laid in waiting to ambush me and those with me when traveling here?"

"How many of you knew about the plans for the ambush or were involved in the planning of it?"

"How many of you were involved with the attempt on Thaddeus Grant's life?"

"How many of you knew about your Commander's uncle the one who grows his grapes and makes wine that if their plan had succeeded that not only Thaddeus Grant who cares for each of you as he would for a son and brother, that Wilford who ministers to many of you in your needs, that Benjamin who has stood up for you on many occasions or me, yes, I know many of you,

How many of you know the identity of the person here supposedly in the palace who took away a community farm from its owner in the Grant Manor estate lands and gave it to your Commanders uncle?"

"I was reminded that many of you are good, that some have softened hearts trying to make a decision, but you have confusion, that there are those whose hearts are hardened and those whose hearts will never change."

"If you were not a participant in any of these acts of treason, then show your honor let your sword fall at your feet and walk off the field now! Many began dropping their swords and walking off the field when everyone who left the field there stood only a hundred and seventy-four including the Commander and a few officers."

"Thaddeus is the Grant of the entire Island of Reconciliation but there is one here GREATER than he! That one went to the cross for you, he bled for you, he died for you, and his enemy thought he had won, on the third day when he arose, his enemy knew that he had lost.
Jesus the Christ the Son of the Living God is alive today and lives in many of your hearts, he is waiting for many of you here today to accept His free gift of salvation. We are saved by grace through faith, humble yourselves and repent of your sin, allowed him into your hearts, be baptized and your life will change."

"YOU have an important decision to make here today, it is not your Commander's decision or his officers, it is your individual decision. Today you will choose to live or die. If you choose to live then you will stand on the ground you are now, and you will die! And if you choose to die to yourself, you will live and walk away, then take the time to kneel and ask the Lord Jesus into your hearts."

"You will choose now and those that stand you will face me and my guard."
One by one they walked away many fell to their knees repenting, many came to the Lord Jesus and were reconciled with God walking on the bridge of reconciliation wrapped in the loving grace of God. Some walked away but did not repent for they were unknowing participants but asked questions and there were those whose hearts were hardened but today they cried repenting.

Less than half remain standing their ground with their arrogant pride blinded by deception. Daniel the Commander of the Grant Manor wanted to take his guard that had come with him to the field to stand with Randolph Grant.

Michael appeared to him and said, "Daniel, be of good cheer your Grant already has a guard standing with him" and he allowed Daniel to see the Grant's Castle Guard that stood behind Randolph Grant. There were thousands upon thousands standing and waiting for his signal which would be pulling the sword that stood in the ground out. Michael said, "It would be better if you and your guard were to pray for those on the field still standing that they would allow for the softening of their heart and their eyes to be open. For Randolph Grant is not done, and he will not pull the sword out of the ground."

Randolph Grant closed his eyes and prayed, "Lord open their eyes and heart to your Word let the blinders that hide the truth be shown to them this day give them the courage to walk off this field. Lord, there must be more than has walked off to be saved in Jesus' name."

Ranulf Grant said, "Randolph Grant pull the sword out of the ground, and we will take this field.

Randolph Grant turned to look at him and said, "the sword that is in the ground was here when I got here, I put it in the ground, and it will not be pulled out of the ground until every chance is given to those who still stand on the field to repent. For I brought the only sword I need, and he said open your eyes and see my armor, then look at the sword that is in my right hand. You will stand ready."

Then the commander of the estate guard said, "We are ready for battle to pull your sword from the ground, or we will charge you."

Randolph Grant turned back and looked at them and said, "Are you in such a hurry to die today. You have less than half your guard still standing with you the brave ones have already left the field, it takes courage to walk away from a fight you cannot win. "

"Look around you, your guard has left your treasonous acts. For they have the honor and courage to walk away from a fight they cannot win. To stand on the side of righteousness rather than unrighteousness. Those that still stand with you are blinded by your empty promises."

"What has your Commander promised you? Has he promised you the sun that sets in the sky, the moon that lights the night, has he promise you honor, that this day you would be remembered by all those on the island, has he promise that you will gain the palace and the island to be your own? I tell you right now what he has promised you are empty promises.

Who, I serve has promised me everlasting life. John 3:16 KJV For God so loved the world, that he gave his only begotten Son, that whosoever believeth in him should not perish, but have everlasting life."

"Romans 10: 9-11 KJV says that if thou shalt confess with thy mouth the Lord Jesus, and shalt believe in thine heart that God hath raised him from the dead, thou shalt be saved. For with the heart man believeth unto righteousness; and with the mouth confession is made unto salvation. For the scripture saith, Whosoever believeth on him shall not be ashamed. Proverbs 16:18 KJV Pride goeth before destruction, and a haughty spirit before a fall."

Their commander said, "We will give you armor then go draw your sword from the ground and step on the field with me."

Randolph Grant said, "I need not your armor made by man. I stand here with the Armor of God. I have the belt of truth, the breastplate of righteousness, my shoes are fitted with the gospel of peace, the shield of faith, the helmet of salvation, and the sword of the Spirit which is the Word of God. I am on the field with you now." The commander stared at him not moving as he turned to his men, many were walking off the field, and as they walked off the field those that had gone before them welcome them one by one kneeling and praying with them.

There was only a handful still on the field and some had tears in their eyes but would not leave the field.

Randolph Grant said, "There is no shame in crying, even Jesus Wept, be courageous." walked off the field and more did. But a few stood their ground.

Michael stood by Randolph Grant and said, "Be of good cheer for many were saved here today by the Word of God."

Randolph Grant looked at Michael with tears streaming from his eyes, "But those that stand will die here today for what?"

Bennet Grant said, "They will be removed from the Island of Reconciliation with no memory of the island and be sent back into the world where with hope and prayer they will find Jesus through faith and repentance. Pull your sword from the ground and let what must be done."

Randolph Grant turned and saw Thaddeus Grant who pulled his sword from the ground and the Grant's Castle Guard swoop across the field with all of them disappearing.

Thaddeus Grant said, "I couldn't pull my sword either when I was confronted with something similar, Benjamin pulled it for me." Thaddeus Grant pulled him to his side hugged him. "You did well here today, I am so proud of you."

Randolph Grant said, "We must talk, you and I alone."

Thaddeus Grant said, "that he and Randolph Grant were going to the garden to talk about today's events."

Wilford asked, "if he would like him and Benjamin to come along?"

Thaddeus Grant said, "no. Tell me, Randolph Grant, why did you want to speak alone? You seem trouble what is wrong? You accomplished a great deal here today for your first day as the Grant of the Manor."

Randolph Grant said, "I don't want to speak ill of any of the Grants who have passed before but why was Ranulf so eager to take the field?"

Thaddeus Grant smiled and said, "He wasn't eager he was testing you to see how you would handle it when someone was trying to be overbearing to you. He would have been proud of how you turned and took command of him."

"Terry Teetson and Burt were lied to by their family or someone else telling them their birthright was stolen that the Island of Reconciliation was theirs."

Thaddeus Grant said, "I know Albert shared with me the same lies. It was the two families that told them the lies. Thora Teetson wanted the second manor because she thought they would get more land when she didn't get it, she and Horace decided to cause problems within their own family with the expectation of causing problems within the island.

How is my young guard John doing?"

Thaddeus Grant replied, "He is with my physician who says he should make a full recovery."

"One of them who were in the fruit trees I have under protective guard. He had a community farm just outside Bennet Village where he grew grapes. He claims that someone from the palace informed him that the community farm was going to be given to someone else. I ask what the name of the person was? He couldn't recall the name but would recognize the person again if he saw the person."

Thaddeus Grant replied, "That he wouldn't see why anyone from the palace would take a community farm away from someone who was on the Grant Manor Estate. What is the name of the person you have in the protective guard?"

Randolph Grant replied, "Neville."

Thaddeus Grant called for a palace guard by the name of Alban and told him, "Two Grant Manor guards have someone in protective guard. Take them and the person through the palace and the grounds to see if he recognizes anyone. He will know what it is about."

The guard Alban said, "Yes sir."

Randolph Grant asked the person with the wine in the private room, "Were you in the room when he came in, or was he there when you came in?"

Thaddeus Grant replied, "I found it odd that he was in the room when he came in. I asked the guards who allowed him to come in. But they didn't even know he was there it was a surprise to them."

Randolph Grant said, "The estate guards who were ready to ambush us that Silas warned us about, how did they know we were coming to the palace? Wilford came to the Manor as requested with two estate guards "why didn't he come with palace guards? When I sent Benji for the ledgers he said Wilford wanted to come back with him. Why would he want to come his duty was to be on the towers?"

Thaddeus Grant asked, "Are you questioning Wilford's loyalty?"

Randolph Grant replied, "I am only asking questions. There is something at play here and I don't know what it is. Why was Benjamin away? Where was he?"

Thaddeus Grant said, "oh he had good news for you when he returned. He had visited with your parents to see if there had been any information in regard to your disappearance."

Randolph Grant replied, "was there?" Thaddeus Grant replied, "I don't know he didn't tell me."

Randolph Grant then asked, "Who was your Butler and Bodyguard when he was away?"

Thaddeus Grant said, "Wilford suggested Ambrose fill in for Benjamin."

Randolph Grant asked, "Where is Ambrose?"

Thaddeus Grant said, "I don't know that is a good question. Let us keep this between us and I will let Benjamin know what we talked about, and you can tell Benji agreed?"

Randolph Grant replied, "Agreed. Thaddeus Grant I am concerned for you. Something is just not right. I would like to leave Daniel, my Commander of my manor guard, on loan as your commander of the Estate Guard until someone is selected to lead them and I would also like for him to select from our guard who has come with him for his officers. Would that be agreeable with you? May I ask also just being curious who would normally select a new Commander?"

Thaddeus Grant replied, "Wilford, I find it hard to believe he would be involved in anything like this? I will take your offer of Daniel and his selection of his guards for officers."

Randolph Grant replied, "I will let Daniel know."

RANDOLPH GRANT JOURNEY HOME

Thaddeus and Randolph Grant walked back from their meeting in the garden. Randolph called for Daniel his Commander of the Grant Manor to come join them. "Daniel I am going to be loaning you to Thaddeus Grant until they select another commander for the estate guard. You will be the temporary Commander until someone has been chosen. You may also select five of our manor guards to be your officers and if you have any questions, you will report only to Thaddeus Grant or Benjamin."

Daniel replied, "Yes sir." He then selected Oliver, Gavin, Thomas, Alexander, and Ethan for his officers. Thaddeus Grant informed the commander of his palace guard to inform the estate guards that Daniel and those he has chosen from the Grant Manor would be his officers.

Randolph Grant asked Samuel and Severin if Neville had seen who had taken his community farm away from him, and they said no. He had them stay with Neville as the guards protected him. He also inquired if his young guard, John, who had been injured was ready to be transported back in a carriage.

Samuel replied that he had seen Doctor Dumpling and Pastor Dumpling helping him into the carriage.

Benji had informed Randolph Grant that he had introduced John, Michael, and Daniel Clacksons to Mr. And Mrs. Dumpling and Randy. Kathryn had told John that she would be able to help him with his stuttering. Randolph Grant wanted to get started back and chose the guards Gunnar and Zachary to make sure everything was secure, and everyone was ready. He also advised that Terry, Terry Jr, Steven, Burt, Neville, and Jonathan all needed guards for the journey back.

As they were getting ready to return Benjamin came running out of the palace calling for Randolph Grant. He said, "I didn't want you to leave before we had a moment to talk about why I was gone and what news I have for you. I had visited with your parents in the world, and they send their love."

Randolph Grant smiled and asked, "How are they? I miss them greatly."

Benjamin said, "They are doing fine, and they miss you as well. He continued to say that they had found out that his friend who was believed to be involved with your disappearance wasn't involved he was cleared. They haven't been able to find who was behind it though."

Randolph Grant said, "Well did you get it?"

Benjamin smiled and said, "No, your mum says she just dumps when she is cooking, so I sat there and watched her cooking, and she just dumps. They both started laughing saying, at the same time, she dumps pretty good when cooking.

Randolph Grant said "Benjamin, keep watch over Thaddeus Grant and don't leave his side. Have all his food and drink tested before he eats or drinks anything."

Benjamin said "Don't worry. I'll keep an eye on him. Have a safe journey back. Have you decided what you're going to do with Terry yet?"

Randolph Grant said, "No." before he climbed into his carriage to begin the trip back to the manor.

Randy asked his mom and dad if he could ride with Mr. Grant because he hadn't seen him in a while.

The guard, William, who was assigned as a guardian for Randy motioned Gunnar to come back to see what was needed.

William asked, "Will you see if Randolph Grant would mind if Randy rode back with him in his carriage for a while."

Gunnar went to see and came back and said, "It would be ok if it is ok with his parents. "

"It is, right?" Randy asked.

His parents nodded yes, and Gunnar put him on his horse and took him to Randolph Grant's carriage.

"Hi Mr. Grant."

Randolph Grant said, "Hi have you enjoyed your trip to the palace?

Randy replied, "Yes, but it is huge. Maybe when we get back to the manor mom's cottage won't be too far away, so I can come to visit you."

Randolph Grant said, "How would you just like to live at the manor?"

Randy, said "Mom and dad too?"

Randolph Grant said, "Yes that would be fine. We have plenty of room. I hear you would like to meet Silas?"

Randy answered with a nod of yes.

"Well, I have a lot of friends who are animals when I was younger. Living here on the Island of Reconciliation I became friends with quite a lot of them."

Randy said, "What other kinds of animals? I saw Jonah, the red fox, on our way here. He had been trapped in a snare and I released him and told him he wouldn't be hurt and that the Grant of the manor had returned."

"I have a feeling that it might have been Lucas who knocked down the tree when I was coming to the palace."

Randy said, "Who is Lucas?"

Randolph Grant smiled and said "Lucas is a bear. I've known him and Catherine his lady bear since they were cubs." As he was telling Randy of all the animals, he had made friends with, they looked up and saw two blue jays, Archibald, and Maribel, landing on the carriage. "Randy, I would like to introduce you to Archibald and Maribel. They are blue jays."

Randy smiled and said "Hello" to Archibald and Maribel. "It's a nice day for flying."

They flew off.

Randy said, "I didn't mean for them to fly off."

Randolph Grant assured him "They don't usually stay around for too long."

Randy said "I see you have Uncle Terry back there. You won't let him bother me, will you?"

Randolph Grant said, "No he's not going to bother you." He began laughing, "Not after your Uncle Burt hit him upside the head when he found out that he didn't tell him your dad, mom, and you were on the island. When he found out Terry hurt you, he punched your Uncle Terry upside the head and told him to never hurt that little guy ever again."

"Which one is Uncle Burt?"

"You don't remember your Uncle Burt?"

"No."

Randolph had the Driver stop the carriage before stepping out. He put Randy on his shoulder, walked back to his mom and dad's carriage explaining what Burt did when he found out that Terry had hurt Randy, he also told them that Burt was excited when he heard that they were also on the island.

Pastor Dumpling said, "Where did you see Burt?"

Randolph Grant replied "He was one of the guests that visited the fruit trees. I thought if you like, I could bring him to your carriage, and all of you could visit with one another for a bit. We're going to be taking a break down here for a bit."

They agreed and Randy said, "Mr. Grant when we're done, can I still ride with you in your carriage?"

Randolph Grant said, "Yes you can."

The guards brought Burt to their carriage, and they were hugging each other. Randolph Grant had one of the guards also bring Jonathan to him as they went over sitting under a tree to talk.

"I checked with my guards, and they all said what you had said checks out. So, I am going to be building a couple of new villages, Tower Houses, cottages, and an animal sanctuary if you are interested. I am going to need a handyman."

Jonathan replied, "Yes sir, I would be greatly interested."

Randolph Grant called Benji over and introduced them and said "When we get back, find out in the Bennet Village and surrounding area who would like to help. Jonathan is going to be the foreman, ok? Until the villages are built, we will provide you and your family with a cottage."

They were getting ready to continue their trip back to the manor. Randolph Grant called Burt and Jonathan over and asked if they were sorry about climbing the wall at the palace. They both said they were, and Burt said, "I remember who you are now, and I'm sorry for how I treated you when I was younger hope, you'll forgive me."

"Burt, I forgave you a long time ago." He called for Benji

"Yes sir."

"Do we have a couple of horses for Burt and Jonathan to ride back on?"

"We can find some."

Randy came over to Randolph Grant and said, "Steven was the one reading my book. He took pretty good care of it. I thought I would let him read it if he promised to give it back the way it is. What do you think?"

"I think it would be a nice gesture and if he did do anything to the book, I've got another one you can have signed by the author."

Randy, said "ok!"

Uncle Burt said "Steven said he wanted to tell his dad what happened, but his brother Terry said not to. So, do you think Steven might be sorry for his part in it?"

Randy said, "I don't know?"

Randolph Grant sent a guard to go get Steven. Steven was walking up to them. He looked scared. When he arrived, he said, "Sir, you wanted to see me?"

Randolph Grant said, "Actually your cousin Randy wanted to ask you something?"

Randy just looked at Mr. Grant and then said, "You took my book."

Steven replied, "Terry took your book, and he was going to mark it all up, but I wanted to read it. It was really interesting. So, I wouldn't let him have it back."

"Uncle Burt said you wanted to tell Uncle Terry what happened, but you didn't because Terry told you not to."

Steven replied "Terry's mean like Dad. I didn't feel like getting beat up. Sorry." He had tears in his eyes fighting desperately to hold them back.

Randy said, "I forgive you and there is no shame in crying. Even Jesus wept. Would you like to continue reading my book?"

Steven said, "Yes it's fascinating."

Randy said, "Come on, I'll get you the book."

Randolph Grant called Randy back and whispered in his ear "You want to see if he wants to ride in the carriage with us while he reads it?"

Randy just looked at Mr. Grant.

Randolph Grant leaned back down and said to him, "You might find kindness and love overcomes a lot of wrongs."

Randy smiled and said, "I'll get the book and Mr. Grant says we can ride with him while you read it ok?"

Steven said, "Really? ok!" Steven looked back at Randolph Grant and said "Why did he do that? I was mean to him."

Randolph Grant said, "Why do you have tears coming from your eyes?"

Steven said "Because, I'm sorry for what I did."

Randolph Grant said, "He sees that and has extended an olive branch of grace unto you by forgiving you. Forgiving someone isn't a sign of weakness it's a strength provided by God's grace."

Randy came back and said "Here, Steven. You ready Mr. Grant?" They went back to the carriage continuing their journey back to the manor.

As Randolph Grant walked with them, he could see Pastor Dumpling and Kathryn smiling. He stopped by the carriage with John his guard to see how he was fairing with the journey back. He was resting in sleep.

As they approached Bennet Village, Neville told the guards, "That's the one there, that took away my community farm."

They picked him up and brought him to Randolph Grant and informed him "This is the man that Neville said came from the palace and took his community farm from him."

Randolph Grant asked, "What is your name?"

The man said "My name is Ambrose, but I know not what this is about? I've never seen this man before who is making this accusation against me."

Randolph Grant then asked, "Have you ever been to the palace?"

Ambrose replied "I've had the privilege to see it from a distance. It is quite beautiful to gaze upon."

"Have you ever been in service to Thaddeus Grant as a temporary Butler?"

Ambrose said, "Thaddeus the Grant of the Island of Reconciliation? Sir it would be such a blessing to even be seen with him but to have been in service to him as a Butler no. I must be on my way now as I have a long journey to return to my home."

Randolph Grant informed him that he wasn't going anywhere until what he had said checked out.

Ambrose said, "Sir, I am a man of my word."

Randolph Grant said "We shall see if you are telling the truth. If you are then you may continue on your journey home. By the way, where is your home?"

"My home is in the Avenskerri Forest some distance from here."

Randolph Grant informed the guards to put him in the guardhouse at the manor in a separate area from the others and do not let them see or talk to him. He then asked for Bethany to be brought to the manor. While all this was going on Benji made the announcement in the village that there would be work for any who would have interest and they would be paid to be at the Grant Manor in the morning.

Home From The Journey

When they arrived at the Grant Manor, they greeted everyone. Randolph Grant informed Jack that he would be taking over the duties as Commander of the Grant Manor Guard until Daniel and the other guards returned from the palace. Bethany, who was an artist, was brought to draw the likeness of Ambrose and Agar and his men to be sent back to Thaddeus Grant to view.

Terry Teetson was placed in the guardhouse away from all the others. Terry and Steven were twelve and ten were placed in the Manor under protective guard while Randolph Grant decided what to do about them and their Dad. Dr. Dumpling checked in on the Clacksons to see how they were fairing with the treatment she had left for them when she traveled to the palace with her family and the guards. The Clackson's health was improving greatly. Michael, Daniel, and John were reunited with them and would stay at the Manor while they recovered. After that time, they would be provided with one of the new cottages that were going to be built.

Jonathan's family was brought to the manor where they would be reunited and would stay at the manor for the evening while a cottage in the Bennet Village was being prepared for them. Benji took Jonathan and Randy to a planning room to wait for Randolph Grant to go over what the plans were for the Grant Manor Estates.

While they were waiting, he had Pastor Dumpling and Kathryn summoned to his private study to discuss Randy's protective guardians and why he provided them.

"Pastor Dumpling and Kathryn, a lot has happened over the last few days. I brought you in to explain why I have protective guardians on Randy. He is a very special young boy, and a path has been chosen for him. It is important that he be kept protected. He had asked if your cottage was close by and if he could come to visit me at the manor. I asked him if he would like to live at the manor? His reply was with mom and dad too? I informed him that would be fine as we have a lot of room here. Would that be suitable for both of you?"

Pastor Dumpling and Kathryn, both said it was agreeable. Randolph Grant also assured Pastor Dumpling he meant what he had said about him mentoring a couple of young men to become ministers to the villages and his offer for him to be the Pastor of Bennet Village.

" Because you will be here at the Grant Manor, I also would like to give you back your given name of Teetson if you would like?"

Pastor Dumpling and Kathryn smiled and said they had discussed it between them and Randy and decided they would like to remain the Dumplings.

Randolph Grant smiled with a giggle said "ok, the Dumplings you will be known as. Kathryn, I know that you are an assistant to my physician, but I would like to offer you the opportunity to be the physician for the estate. We will be expanding and building more villages with cottages, there will also be some tower houses built along with certain areas of the grounds. I will also be adding an animal sanctuary for their safety. There will be a search made for the right area."

Kathryn said, "I would love to accept the opportunity."

"There is one other issue that I believe you both should know. I know the biological parents of Randy. Jackson, and Ally are friends of mine in the world. It was shared with me how you came about becoming the Adopted Parents of Randy."

Kathryn said "We didn't know of any details. Wilford brought a young child to me and asked me to become the mother and that the parents had passed on."

Randolph Grant replied "That is not how it was told to me. Wilford? Why would he tell you one thing and me another? There is going to need some clarification on this matter that I am going to have checked out. For now, keep it between us, so I can look into this."

Pastor Dumpling said, "He is our child."

Randolph Grant said "I know that. There is the truth that needs to be found out regarding this situation for Wilford had told me that when Randy was older that you would share with him his parent's love for him and their sacrifice to keep him protected."

Kathryn said, "He never said anything like that to me. Are you going to have him come here to explain all of this?"

Randolph Grant said "No, I am going to have it looked into. I have sources for such things. It will be fine. I have a meeting to go to with Benji and Jonathan. Randy is there with them in the planning room. Would both of you like to come to the meeting to give advice and feedback on what we're going to be doing?"

They both said yes.

"Theo?"

"Yes sir?"

"Could you take the Dumplings to the planning room?"

Theo replied, "Yes sir."

He then met with Arthur and Finley advising them to have their teams check into the matter they had discussed before meeting the Dumplings.

Theo, a staff member who assisted Benji at the manor, had returned from taking the Dumplings to the planning room that Randolph Grant was heading to.

Randolph Grant motioned for Theo and then asked, "By any chance did Bethany bring Logan with her today?"

Theo smiled and "Yes sir, he is in the kitchen area. Rachel is making him some cinnamon bread."

"Could you ask him when he is done enjoying his treat if he could bring Silas to me, and maybe you could accompany him and don't forget to get you some sweet treat that Rachel is cooking."

"Yes sir."

Randolph Grant was on his way to the planning room, but he was still troubled by Wilford telling him one thing and Kathryn something totally different.

Michael met him in the hallway and said "Be of good cheer Randolph Grant. The answers you seek can be found in the towers."

Randolph Grant asked Michael "Are you an Angel?"

Michael replied, "I am blessed to be the messenger of the Grant Manor and have waited for the Grant to return to the manor, and you are the Grant of Grace for you are the fifth. You have many wrongs that have been done to make right and help to bring peace on the Island of Reconciliation." Michael then disappeared.

Randolph Grant wanted to immediately go to the towers to find the answers, but he realized the towers are normal straight up and down towers. What mysterious clue has Michael provided?

He finally entered the planning room where Benji, Jonathan, Randy, Pastor Dumpling, and Kathryn were waiting. Benji and Kathryn both could tell something was adrift with him, but he wasn't letting onto anything.

Randolph Grant greeted them and said "Well, I have some ideas. I would like to add to the Grant Manor." On the large square table in the middle of the room were the estates as they appeared currently. "There are some community farms beyond the Bennet Village, and I would like to open the area for more. There are a lot of lands that can be used to help feed everyone living within the estate lands. The main road, leading past the Bennet Village, will split off into two roads. The one on the left will go for the community farms and the one to the right will need to have more cottages built to house those that will be tending different types of gardens for vegetables, flowers and more fruit trees planted behind the cottages. I also want tower houses built going down each of these roads and at the end of the road, there will need to be a gatehouse for entry.

"Going back to the Bennet Village there is a road that leads out toward the forest area. This area, I also plan to develop for use. There will be two splits to the right and left at each split there will be tower houses built. The first right will be to add more cottages for gardens, the second right will be for community farms. The first left and second will lead to smaller manors for the elderly. At the end of the main road, there will be another Gatehouse built for entry.

Over here by the Grant Manor, down the boundary pass, the apple trees, the road will split one to the left and the other to the right for two more villages to be built. At the end of the main road will be a gatehouse and off to each side tower houses. There also is going to be a search for an animal sanctuary to keep the animals safe. At Harborshire, fish and other goods can be purchased. Any thoughts?"

Jonathan said "It will be a big undertaking. Where would you like to start first?"

"The Bennet Village side first. Phase 1: The community farms plot of land will be divided into a few hundred parcels for individuals to grow food plants. There is a community farm that was taken from a man named Neville. That will be returned to him. They'll also need cottages built for them. Whatever seed is needed, Benji you can send those to Harborshire to buy it."

Benji, said, "Yes sir, and we can also get the seed for the garden vegetables."

Randolph Grant replied, "Yes that will be Phase 2. Phase 3 is to complete those sections. We will need two tower houses and the gatehouse building. After those phases are completed, we'll move towards the other side of Bennet Village."

Benji said," We have the villagers from Bennet Village arriving in the morning."

Randolph Grant looked at Jonathan "You are in charge, let Benji know what you need."

Jonathan said "Can I stay here reviewing everything to get the best idea?

Randolph Grant replied "Yes."

Pastor Dumpling said, "Suggestion. How about a church in the village for the elderly?"

Randolph Grant replied, "Yes and Kathryn, do you know of any medical helpers for those areas?"

Kathryn replied, "Yes."

Randy said, "I have a suggestion."

Everyone looked at Randy and said what is it?

"How about a school?"

Randolph Grant said, "Yes! Jonathan take the time you need. Benji can stay with you, and I'll send you some aides to help."

Pastor Dumpling said, "I would like to stay too if that would be, ok?"

Randolph Grant said, "That's fine. Randy, I've sent for someone you wanted to meet would you like to go see if he has arrived yet?"

Randy said, "Who?"

Randolph Grant said, "Silas."

Kathryn said, "Can I go too? I haven't seen Silas in some time."

Randy said, "ok."

Randolph Grant, Kathryn, and Randy went to see if Theo and Logan were back yet with Silas. They walked to one of the most beautiful private gardens from the back of the manor. The reddish cobblestone led them to where there were lush greens and trees with flowers of all kinds planted by the trees there were fountains and blue-stone benches where they all sat down to wait for Theo, Logan, and Silas to visit them.

Randy and Kathryn both could tell something else was on Randolph Grant's mind, Kathryn wondered if it was about what they had discussed when she and her husband were in the room regarding Randy but wouldn't ask while Randy was with them.

Randy said, "Mr. Grant what's the matter?"

His mom said, "Mr. Grant has a lot of responsibilities that he must think about often."

Randy said, "Like what?"

Randolph Grant smiled and laughed about his question. He then turned and saw Theo, Logan, and Silas making their way down the cobblestone path towards them. Once they arrived, Randolph Grant introduced Theo and Logan to Kathryn and

Randy. Silas jumped in Randolph Grant's lap and climbed up and laid down on his shoulder.

Randolph Grant said, "Silas, I have a friend that I would like to introduce you to."

Silas raised up and looked at him.

"Silas, this is Randy, Kathryn's son."

Silas looked at Randy and said, "Hello Mr. Randy."

Randy's eyes opened wide with a surprised look all over his face. He looked at his mom and said, "He can talk?"

They all started laughing because not too many on the Island of Reconciliation had the gift to hear when the animals actually spoke, they would only hear the animal noises they would make. It was a blessing not to be shared with those who didn't know.

Kathryn told Randy that he was blessed and told him why.

Silas said, "All the animals were glad when they learned that you were the Grant. How can I be of service to you?"

Randolph Grant asked, "Where are all the animals?"

Silas replied "They are afraid to come out because there are those who have tried to harm them. Michael introduced us to two of his messengers who warn us of any danger. Those that your guards took out of Bennet Village were very cruel to many of our friends who are no more."

Randy said, "Mr. Grant is going to take care of that for all of you." Silas said, how? Randolph Grant said we're going to find a place on the Island of Reconciliation on Grant Manor for a sanctuary for you and all your friends. Silas said, where? Who are the messengers that Michael introduces you to?

Silas said, "Elizabeth and Charlotte have been able to keep us safe by warning us. "

Randolph said "Theo."

"Yes sir."

"Go to the commander, Jack, and tell him that I would like for Samuel and Severin to join us here. Then you come back too."

Theo said, "Yes sir, I'll hurry back."

Kathryn asked, "What are you going to do?"

"I don't know?" He bowed his head and said, "Father in Heaven please help us with this matter in Jesus' name."

Silas said "It's a shame that Mr. Habens isn't on the Island of Reconciliation. He is very knowledgeable of the island. He was Alistair Grant's Butler. When Alistair Grant passed on Mr. Habens wasn't around anymore. He talked to all the animals, and we heard that Wilford said he left the island one day and didn't know where he went."

Randy said, "Mr. Habens is at Harborshire on the pier he tells everyone that they need faith to come to the Island of Reconciliation."

Theo returned with Samuel and Severin, "Sir, you wanted to see us?"

Randolph Grant sat there with a dazed stare on his face thinking, *who is Wilford*? He raised up and said, "Yes, sorry. I have something for both of you to do." He walked a distance away from everyone with them. "I need for both of you to go to Harborshire and bring Mr. Habens back secretly to the manor. Inform the commander that you are on a mission for me."

They both said, "Yes, sir."

Severin said, "What if he won't come back?"

"Find out why?"

Michael was standing by the fountain and Randolph Grant walked over to him.

Michael said "Be of good cheer Randolph Grant. Mr. Habens will not come back."

"Why?"

"He has been told that the only way he can come back is if a Grant tells him to blow his horn and then he will have the faith needed to step on the bridge. If he blows the horn, he will be in danger that he doesn't know about."

"Who told him that?"

"You will find your answers in the towers."

"Do you know of a place where the animals can be safe?"

"They only need to come to the Grant Manor, and they will be safe."

"Listen to hear the voice in your spirit on how to bring Mr. Habens back home."

Randolph Grant smiled at Michael. "Thank you, Lord Jesus, for answered prayer. Silas let all your friends know to come home to the Manor."

He ran after Samuel and Severin and when catching them said "Forget what I have asked of you. Find me Pastor Dumpling. He may still be in the Planning Room."

"Yes sir."

As he said that, Pastor Dumpling was walking towards them. "I need your help." and he explained to him what he needed. Pastor Dumpling said, "I will return with him."

"Albert, do you want me to send any guards with you?"

Pastor Dumpling said, "I already have my guard with me." and he smiled.

Michael returned and introduced Elizabeth and Charlotte to Randolph Grant.

They said "Be of good cheer. We are alerting the animals to come home." They then told Randolph Grant where they would be at when he would like to visit.

"I would like to put a gatehouse there to stop any entrance to those who would cause harm."

They all returned to the Manor where Randolph Grant went to his private study and awaited the arrival of Mr. Habens. He wondered what Michael had said about his answers would be found in the towers, and he looked up and down the tower in his study but found nothing. He was growing tired from all the activities for the day when Benji, Kathryn, and Randy came to see him with Silas laying on Randy's shoulder.

They all wanted to know where Pastor Dumpling had gone. Randy wanted to know who it was back at the fountain that he had been talking to, he said he recognized Michael but wondered who the other two ladies were. Benji and Kathryn were dumbfounded because they hadn't seen anyone by the fountain with him thinking he was just in thought. Silas knew but kept quiet for if Randolph Grant wanted to say he would.

Randolph Grant asked Benji if we had any treats for Silas?

Benji replied, "I believe we can find some for him,"

Silas raised his head up off of Randy's shoulder that he had been resting on and looked at Benji who left the room with Silas to go look for some treats.

Randolph Grant looked at Kathryn and then asked a question of Randy that didn't have anything to do with his question of who was by the fountain with him. "Randy, tell me everything that you can remember about the Island of Reconciliation for my understanding is that you once lived here with your mom and dad before they left and went into the world. Do you have any memories of before then?"

Kathryn glanced back at Randolph Grant in amazement that he had asked the question. (For she knew the answer that he would find in the Towers but couldn't say anything.)

Randy replied, "I have been having some dreams, but I don't know what they mean."

Randolph Grant asked, "What are the dreams you are having?"

Randy said, "There is a beautiful lady who was crying because someone had forcibly taken her child from her. Then she is crying joyfully because an older man and woman brought her child back to her. Mom, why would someone be so cruel to do that to someone? She is beautiful like you."

Kathryn held him in her arms and said "I don't know why people are cruel like that to others. Kathryn began crying for she knew who the woman was that received her child back and who the older man and woman were that brought the child back to her.

Kathryn said, "Randy let me know if you have any more dreams about them or let Mr. Grant know.

Randy replied, "ok. Mr. Grant, who was standing by the fountain with you and Michael?"

Mr. Grant (Randolph Grant) said to Randy "It was two of Michael's messengers Charlotte and Elizabeth. They were going to help keep Silas and his friends safe."

Randy said, "They were beautiful."

Randolph Grant had looked up while Kathryn and Randy were talking and saw his blubbering friend Benji in the hallway. He had overheard what was being said and entered the room.

Benji said to Randy "Would you like to come to help me with the treats for Silas?

Randy jumped up and said "ok."

Benji knew that Randolph Grant and Kathryn needed to talk quietly.

Randolph Grant said to Kathryn "You're pretty good with dreams what do you think of Randy's dream?"

Kathryn said, "There is a mother whose son was taken and given back to her."

Randolph Grant only looked at Kathryn knowing she was holding something back because he knew her but didn't say anything. "I asked Albert to go bring back Mr. Habens who I hope will be able to fill in the answers or even help me with finding where they are?"

Mr. Habens Comes Home

Pastor Dumpling got in his carriage and drove it to the Bridge
of Reconciliation. With faith he was on the bridge heading back
to Harborshire to bring back Mr. Habens, who was standing on
the pier dejected because he was unable, by faith, to step on the
bridge to tell Pastor Dumpling he didn't have to do an act of
kindness. Every time he had tried to take a step of faith, doubt
and fear would become an obstacle and he would step off the
pier landing in the water.

Pastor Dumpling had parked the carriage and walked toward
Mr. Habens. He asked, "Why are you so downcast Mr. Habens?"

He looked up he saw the Pastor and said "Oh, I am so glad
you came back. You didn't have to do an act of kindness after
you and your young son took your ride of faith. I saw a notation
that your name had been changed from Teetson to Dumpling.
Every time I would try to take a step of faith on the bridge I
landed in the water. The only way I can go back is if a Grant on
the Island of Reconciliation tells me to blow the horn that was

given to me and then I would see the island and bridge to cross it."

Pastor Dumpling said "God has plans for us and He plans the steps for us. We may put plans in motion by our own will or even by accident, but God still plans the steps for us. Although there were some circumstances from you giving me an act of kindness to do, it all worked out. I used to live on the Island of Reconciliation and left. When I came back with my son it was to reconcile with my wife who was on the island. I never made it to the act of kindness you had provided. Instead, a little red squirrel blocked my path and I instead traveled to Bennet Village where I was able to reconcile with the villagers because I was a bully when I was younger. I also was able to preach to a large group and was forgiven by someone whom I bullied when I was younger. Yes, my son and I found my wife and his mother, and we were able to reconcile as well. So, everything worked together for the good of those who are the called and who love the Lord.

"Now. I have been asked to bring you back to the Island of Reconciliation and you do not need anyone to tell you that you can come back or to blow a horn to see the Island of Reconciliation and step on the Bridge of Reconciliation. All you need is what you have and that is faith in God. You do not need to have faith in the bridge only knowing and believing by faith in the Lord Jesus."

Mr. Habens said, "It is nice what you have said but unless a Grant tells me to blow the horn I am not allowed to come."

Pastor Dumpling said, "Who has told you this?"

Thaddeus Grant Island Of Reconciliation

"The Butler of Thaddeus Grant warned me not to come back until a Grant said I could. He said that I am responsible for what happened to Alistair Grant." Mr. Habens began to cry and said, "I didn't do anything to hurt him. Wilford said I had to wait for the Grant to blow the horn to come back. It must be true because I have tried so many times to step on the bridge to return home."

Pastor Dumpling said, "Wilford is not Thaddeus Grant's butler and never has been his butler. Benjamin is Thaddeus Grant's butler, bodyguard, and friend. Thaddeus Grant believes in reconciliation, not in sowing fear and doubts into someone as you have had done to you. Answer me now. Do you love the Lord Jesus the Christ the Son of the Living God?"

Mr. Habens said, "With all my heart."

"Do you believe He went to the cross so that you could be forgiven and have eternal life through him?"

Mr. Habens replied, "Yes."

"Is he your savior or is Wilford?"

Mr. Habens said, "Jesus is my Savior."

Pastor Dumpling said, "Then let us get in the carriage and take a ride of faith together, with faith all things are possible."

Mr. Habens climbed into the carriage with Pastor Dumpling and the horses began to pull the carriage into a gallop off the pier. When Mr. Habens opened his eyes, he saw the beautiful reddish cobblestone Bridge of Reconciliation and his horses had turned white as snow. He began to cry and grab a hold of Pastor Dumpling, hugging him and thanking him for his kindness. They both praised the Lord all the way to the Grant Manor.

Mr. Habens noticed things did not seem right. For he was Alistair Grant's butler and historian for the Island of Reconciliation. He asked, "Will we see Thaddeus Grant now?"

Pastor Dumpling said, "We are going to see the Grant of the Manor who asked me to come and to get you, to bring you home.

Mr. Habens said, "Who is that?"

Pastor Dumpling replied, "Randolph Grant."

Mr. Habens asked, "Is Thaddeus Grant no longer alive?"

Pastor Dumpling said, "He is very much alive, but he is at a palace in another province."

Mr. Habens then asked, "How many Grants are there?"

Pastor Dumpling could tell something must be awry because of all his questions. He said "Thaddeus Grant is the Grant of the Island of Reconciliation, the one who will succeed him is the fifth Grant and he is the Grant that has returned to the manor. We will be there soon, and Randolph Grant will answer any questions you have."

When they arrived at the manor, Benji greeted them, and Silas flew into Mr. Habens. He was very excited to see him and was crawling all over him welcoming him back and telling him that he missed him so much. Mr. Habens was just as joyful to see his friend.

Benji took Pastor Dumpling, Mr. Habens, and Silas to Randolph Grant's private study where he, Kathryn, and Randy were still chatting. After all the introductions. Randolph Grant asked that everyone to let him and Mr. Habens talk privately with one another. Before leaving Pastor Dumpling told him about his talk with Mr. Habens and what Wilford had done.

Randolph Grant said, "Hello Mr. Habens. I remember you when my family and I left many years ago and you told me that God would help me if I only believed and asked for his help."

Mr. Habens said, "I remember you, Jackson Randolph." and smiled. "I am confused why Thaddeus Grant is not here in the palace and the Pastor said that he is in what must be another palace?"

Randolph Grant said, "Something is not right, and I don't know what it is? I think the lies are catching up with Wilford and I don't know who he is."

Mr. Habens said "All I can tell you in regard to him is that I didn't find him in the historical visitor logs that were kept by all the Grants, and I told Alistair Grant about it. I was sent off on an errand by the palace Commander and when I got back Alistair Grant had passed on and Thaddeus Grant was chosen as the Grant. Then the palace Commander said that I would need to speak to his butler who I was introduced to me as Wilford. He said that Thaddeus Grant was removing me from the Island of Reconciliation, and I would be stationed at Harborshire, and you know the rest of that story."

Randolph Grant asked, "Did he word it as reconciliation island and not the Island of Reconciliation?"

Mr. Habens said "He said reconciliation island which I thought was odd because it's always been pronounced as the Island of Reconciliation.

I've been told I can find the answers that I am searching for in the towers. I have not seen anything in any of the towers. The only thing I can think of it must be something called The Towers.

Didn't Thaddeus Grant tell you where the towers are?"

Randolph Grant shook his head no. "When I first met Thaddeus Grant, it was at this manor and when I left and came back there had been another palace built in another province.

Mr. Habens asked, "What province?"

"Airdrocks."

Mr. Habens said with concern, "Has there been an attempt to take that palace and kill Thaddeus Grant?"

"There was an attempt made by the Commander of the Estate Guard, but it failed."

Mr. Habens said, "They will try again."

Randolph Grant said, "Who will try again?"

"The Avenskerri are from the island of deception that was trying to take the Island of Reconciliation. Ranulf Grant was injured at the battle on the field of Airdrocks. They will select another commander who will bring their guards together."

Randolph Grant said, "No, they won't. I have already left my commander of the Randolph Grant Manor there with five of my guards that Daniel selected himself for his officers."

Michael was standing in the hallway and said "Be of good cheer Mr. Habens and Randolph Grant. Mr. Habens you can trust Randolph Grant as he is the Grant of Grace, and he will serve the Grant Manor as it has been called since a time when the deception was made against Thaddeus Grant. Who, by the way, is aware of what is going on? He has been trying to find the link and I told Randolph Grant the answers would be found in The Towers."

Randolph Grant looked at Mr. Habens and said, "Welcome home, now tell me where The Towers are, and will you be my historian?"

Mr. Habens said, "Yes I will." He then showed him the Grant's towers that were in the treasure room under the large table where Thaddeus Grant's most precious gem had sat but now Randolph Grant's most precious gem sat. When you move it to the right of the table, the entranceway will open to the Towers of the Grant's. They entered the first level of The Towers.

The Grant Towers History

Michael was there to greet them. "Be of good cheer Randolph Grant and Mr. Habens. Welcome to the Towers of the Grants. Randolph Grant, allow me to introduce the messengers for each Grant tower to you and your historian Mr. Habens."

Messengers Of The Towers

1. Noah is the messenger for the Ranulf Grant Tower,

2. Jacob is the messenger for the Bennet Grant Tower,

3 Reuben is the messenger for the Alistair Grant Tower,

3a Hope is the messenger for the *Kingston Grant Tower,

4 Joseph is the messenger for the Thaddeus Grant Tower

5 Isaac Is the messenger for the Randolph Grant Tower and

Thaddeus Grant Island Of Reconciliation

5a Arabella is the messenger for the Evan Randolph Grant Tower.

The palace that Thaddeus Grant has had built is a false palace which he is aware of. Once all the Castellan are removed from the Island of Reconciliation the false palace will be destroy. The manor in which you're standing is the rightful palace of the Grants. As we are going over the history if you have any questions, please feel free to asked them."

"Oh, I have questions as well as suspicions." Said Randolph Grant

"By God's grace, your answers will be here, and everything will be made right again."

"Do we have a room that we can go to? I like to ponder and think on the information that is going to be provided and I would like some parchment to write down questions and thoughts."

"Yes, let's go in the study, there is a large table with chairs for you to be comfortable."

RANULF GRANT HISTORY

"Ranulf Grant came to the Island of Reconciliation, and he met a Castellan who was here to claim the islands. Ranulf Grant told him to get off his island and that he had purchased the Island of Reconciliation and all the lands that came with it.

"The Castellan left only to return years later after Ranulf, and his people had built and mapped the island. He saw the islands that lay beyond the Island of Reconciliation that he named:

1. Island of Redemption
2. Island of Peacefulness
3. Island of Joyfulness
4. Island of Grace
5. Island of Strength
6. Island of Transformation
7. Island of Kindness

"They built cottages on all the Islands for those who wished to stay once they visited to reconcile with those here that they had differences with. While on the Island of Transformation Ranulf could see another larger landmass that he had not seen before. It was a far distance away. He had a ship built that would carry more of his men and set sail for the landmass.

"It was a beautiful forest of lush greens and woods and a mountain range where a large Oak tree was all by itself. There was no path to walk to get to the top of the mountain to view what was there. Ranulf was a very husky and big man, with a determination he climbed to the top and could see all the islands. He would make his first mistake that would be costly by not listening to the Oak tree."

"Who asked him why he climb to the top of his mountain?"

There was no response from Ranulf it wasn't that he didn't hear what was said, it was because he chose not to hear the question from the Oak tree. Ranulf was enamored with the view and all he could think on was building a Castle so he could view all his islands and he did.

"He soon made his second crucial mistake that would change everything. He claimed the forest as his own. The forest was not part of the Island of Reconciliation, this forest was a mysterious forest that belonged to the Guardians. They protected the forest, what were the mysteries? We do not know. The forest name would be changed to be known as the Forest of Battleton and this would be his third mistake, for it was not for him to change the name.

"The name change did not sit well with the Guardians, the renaming of their forest displeased them greatly, their kind is peaceful, unless provoke, the Oak tree wasn't happy as well with what was happening so much that the wind blew through the Willow Trees sending a message for the Guardians to come in force to defend their forest that was being taken.

"There was already a large number of Guardians within the forest. The Guardians were there in large numbers showing the mysteries of the forest to their young prince and princess Guardians. Their Queen had travel with them, along with Queen Warriors, Prince Warriors, and Princess Warriors as guards for the younger prince and princesses who were young children.

"The Castellan, whose name was Caselton, came back with his army demanding that Ranulf leave his forest known as the Forest of Avenskerri. With his arrogance he thanked Ranulf for building such a castle on the mountain range to allow for him to view all his islands.

"Ranulf once again informed him the Island of Reconciliation and all the lands about the island were his lands, and for him to leave. Ranulf was outnumbered having a small number of guards with him. The Guardians Queen Warrior Ekatherina viewed from a distance to see what this large man was going to do, who had trample on their forest. She already knew what they were going to do in regard to Caselton, for his kind was their arch enemy and they were not going to allow for him to take their forest, even if it meant standing with Ranulf in battle against Caselton.

The fight was fierce between Ranulf and the Castellan.

Queen Warrior Ekatherina ordered the Guardians to join forces with Ranulf to push back the Castellan and his army of Avenskerri. The Castellan called for more reinforcements. His Avenskerri now outnumbered both Ranulf guards and the Guardians.

Ranulf fearing for his guard's safety called for a retreat to the Islands of Strength, Transformation, and Kindness.

"Ranulf Guards were able to hold off the Avenskerri from reaching the islands with the help of the Guardians giving Ranulf the numbers he needed to withstand any assault from the Castellan."

"Ranulf showed no kindness towards the Guardians who without their help he no doubt would have become no more. The Guardians lost a great deal of their warriors in the incursion, leaving them with mostly the young princes and princesses with a small number of mature warriors.

"We all fall short of the Glory of God making mistakes. We all sin, even though we are saved, for anyone who says they don't have sin, then God's word says they are liars. There is only one who had no sin and he stretched out his arms on the Cross of Calvary so we could be forgiven to receive eternal life by the grace of God through his son Jesus. This is no excuse for Ranulf actions for they were misguided by whoever told him all the lands were his and not informing of which lands were actually his."

"This Caselton character, who is this dude anyway? Is there still a threat from his kind against the Island of Reconciliation? Wherever this forest is that will need to be returned to the Guardians as well as the name of the forest receiving its original name once again restored." Said, Randolph Grant."

"Wilford's name used to be Caselton until Thaddeus Grant changed it to Wilford. The Castellan are from the Island of Deception, they have taken a human form from someone's likeness, they are spirits of deception who must be removed from the Island of Reconciliation to begin the process of healing. There are those on the islands who are not of their kind but are full of just as much deception. Ranulf Grant cries in the Gatehouse of Gideon for his actions. Pride goeth before a fall. He will fall later in his history; it will be from deception." Said, Noah the messenger for Ranulf Grants history."

"So is the Caselton in the time of Ranulf, is he Wilford in this era of time?"

"We believe so."

"What is the rest of the history?"

"Once Ranulf returned to the Island of Reconciliation his concerned grew because the Guardians outnumbered his guards. He made another mistake in judgment instead of showing kindness and gratitude for their help, he set a trapped for when the guardians would come to the Island of Reconciliation by small numbers imprisoning them. First the smaller children came and were separated into groups being sent to different areas of the Island of Reconciliation under the guard of his commanders."

"They were ordered by Ranulf not to use their guardian names. Commanders renamed them, others were given the option to choose another name, which displeased the three Princesses who were in line to become the next queen of the guardians. Once Ranulf had all the children scattered abroad, he then allowed for the more mature warriors to come to the Island of Reconciliation whose Ranulf guards outnumbered sending them to the guardhouse.

"There was a so-called peace established between Ranulf and the Guardians that was brokered by Guardians Princess Erisante and Prince Krastinock. The Guardians would be ruled by Princess Erisante and the Prince Krastinock who assured Ranulf there would be no issues, they would select who would lead each group that had been separated and it would be best advise to allow them to keep their Guardian names so the other Guardians would know they were the leaders, and the Guardians weapons would be taken from them."

Randolph Grant reached for a sheet of parchment and ink and quill writing a note then sign with his signature with his signet ring.

"Michael, have a messenger ride with David with this urgent note to be given to Thaddeus's Grant only, wait for his reply, then return it to me and only me."

Michael said, "I will take care of it at once. May I ask what you have written Randolph Grant?"

"Although I have the authority here at the Grant Manor to make decisions. I would need Thaddeus Grant's permission to make the changes to correct the wrongs that have been done to the Guardians."

"I will take care of it at once. Arabella reached out to David the eagle letting him know we need his assistance on an urgent matter for Randolph Grant. Have the young messenger, Luke, ready to ride an eagle."

"Arabella, I'll let you know when he has arrived."

"Continue with this sorry tell of abuse towards the Guardians. Michael one other thing first, if you believe that Wilford is this Caselton why do you just not have the messenger guard send him back to his world without knowledge of the Island of Reconciliation?"

"We tried this once for we had the same thought. They just sent another to replace the one who the Messenger Guard removed. That is how we got Wilford."

"What else do we have in this sordid history?"

Arabella came into the room saying, "Be of good cheer... David and Luke are on their way to Thaddeus Grant. David said he will be back as quickly as they can."

"Thank you, Arabella," said Randolph Grant.

"Ranulf Grant was devastated that he lost his Castle on the high mountain in the forest. When they had mapped the Island of Reconciliation, they had discovered other castles that had been built within the mountains.

"There were three mountain ranges that were close by one another seemingly joined together that had Castles built within them. Each Castle had a name engraved on them. The castle that Ranulf declare as his had the name Traffanti engraved on it. Ranulf had the engraving removed and his name engraved on the Castle declaring the name of the Castle and mountain as Everard. He then had the other names engraved on the other castles within the other mountains removed as well. Those names were Banitai and Craveranti.

"A remnant of the families of the Ranulf Grant palace Guards were sent there for safety.

"Ranulf asked me to protect the Castle with tears in his eyes. I assured him I would. "I have the Messengers Guard protecting the Castle and the Families living there."

Randolph Grant shook his head in unbelief.

Noah the messenger for the Ranulf Grant history asked, "Randolph Grant is there something that you would like to share regarding what has been said about the castles in the mountains? I ask because you have fresh ears hearing and eyes seeing the history. I believe you to be wise and maybe you are hearing something or seeing something that we are not or have and could help you with understanding."

"Well Noah, I find it to be amazing that he was only devastated with losing his Castle on the mountain and not the forest or what trespass of wrongs against the Guardians. Then regarding the castles in the mountains, he asked for the castles to be protected but doesn't mention the families? It is just an ironic situation. Do you have any history of Ranulf before he purchased the Island of Reconciliation and the lands that pertain to them? It could shed a light on why he is how he is."

Michael said, "Yes, there is history before he purchased the Island of Reconciliation and all the lands pertaining them. This is not in his history here, but I can share it with you on why he seems to be the way he is.

"Ranulf arrived at Harborshire from his world where he had been abused emotional by his brothers and friends. He has four brothers, he doesn't claim any of them, three are bad and one is good. He likes the good one whose name is Elijah who is a minister of the Lord Jesus. Who would tell him to pray for them, but they never changed?? Ranulf has chosen not to claim any of them. His other brothers have always taken advantage of him.

- Reignerand Everard – who is a lover of power, always tried taking control of him with verbal, physical, and emotional abusive behaviors......
- Randal Everard- who is a lover of lies, lie about him causing great embarrassment many times over.
- Rinanthan Everard – who was a lover of lust of riches, stole from him.

"Elijah told him of the Island of Reconciliation saying it would be a good place for him to escape them with a break from all their antics towards him. He came here to escape them all. Ranulf was very wealthy, he fell in love with the peace of the Island of Reconciliation, when he heard it was for sale, he bought it all joyfully. The original owner did not tell him of the history or the troubles, nor about the Messengers. It was a good question, Randolph Grant.

"Well, now I understand his behavior, it doesn't make it right though. That's the thing about people who don't understand someone's behavior. They cannot see the hidden scars that others inflict upon them. Unless they share them with those who care about them and get help. I understand him to a degree for I experience similar situations. It is only by God's grace of healing in my life that I can see his behavior with understanding."

"Ranulf fall came by deception from the Castellan who is the deceiver masquerading as a messenger with lies and deception. Who constantly provided advice for him to pull his guards from the Island of Redemption and the surrounding Islands. The deceiver assured that the Castellan army was much smaller than when they first fought their battle in the forest that he could set a trap where they could pull them into the Airdrocks Valley and crush them. It was all a deception to allow the enemy onto the Island of Reconciliation to fight where the Castellan would have a greater advantage.

"Ranulf had shared the information with Bennet Bantam, a young man who seem to be blessed with wisdom. They talked about a strategy to end this fight once and for all. When they were ready, they put the plan into motion. It was a very costly mistake and one that would cost him his life and many others.

"They created two tunnels one that would bring them within three miles of the Airdrocks Valley by his palace Guards on horseback. The second tunnel brought them within the same distance, allowing their archers to go to the mountains, and the guards on foot would join Ranulf forces.

"Ranulf and a small number of palace guards would arrive at the Airdrocks Valley. Given the illusion that they were small to spring the trap on the Castellan and his army.

"When they were ready, Bennet was to lead the attack from the tunnel with the palace guards on horseback, and a palace guard, Archibald was to join Ranulf Grant on the field, and the archers would make their way to the mountain.

"The signal was to come from the false messenger, the signal never came. Bennet and Archibald's armies were in the tunnels while Ranulf was being slaughtered on the field by the Castellan army."

"Ranulf had been severely injured, he said that there was a will for who the lands were to be left too, before passing on to the Gatehouse of Gideon some had heard him say Elijah who was his brother whom he never claimed. When the will was found to everyone's surprise the Island of Reconciliation and it's lands were not left to Elijah, but to Bennet who would become the second Grant succeeding Ranulf?"

"Do you have the will? If so, I would like to see it."

Noah brought the will to Randolph Grant who looked over it. It looked legit. He handed it to Mr. Habens for him to scour over it to see if he could find anything out of sorts with it.

"So, who is next in the history Michael?" Said, Randolph Grant.

"Bennet Grant History will be next Randolph Grant."

Mr. Habens said, "hmm."

He then picked up the will placing it almost all the way on his face.

"What are you doing Mr. Habens?" Said Randolph Grant with a smile.

"Scouring the will as you said to do. I cannot make out what this extremely tiny print is at the bottom of the will? This marked in the designed I have seen it someplace before but can't recall where."

"Let me see where you are looking at? Maybe my younger eyes can make out what is written. That is tiny, if I was back in my world, I could put a magnifying glass on it to see what it says." Said Randolph Grant.

"What is a magnifying glass?" Asked Mr. Habens.

"If you put it on something it makes it bigger so you can read it."

"I would like to have one of those." Said Mr. Habens.

Right now, I would like to have one Mr. Habens," said Randolph Grant laughing.

Noah said, "May I see what you are looking at? OH NO! How could this have been missed?"

"What do you see," said all three of them at once.

Noah said, "It says 'By Order of Caselton, the Castellan of the Avenskerri'."

Michael said, "Let me see the will. Where are you looking at?"

Noah showed him where Mr. Habens had seen the tiny print.

"THE WILL IS FALSE!" Said Michael. "Mr. Habens what mark in the design did you see that you can't recall?"

Mr. Habens showed Michael the mark. Michael's head fell in disbelief that it had not been seen before now. It was what was on Wilford's signet ring for communication with staff at the palace.

Randolph Grant said, "I would like to speak to the palace guard Archibald is he still alive?"

Noah said, "He is no more, he was heartbroken by what happened to Ranulf Grant. He asked to be able to join the families at the castle in the Everard Mountains, which was granted. He was found a few days later with an arrow in him. One that no one had seen before."

"Do you have the arrow? I would like to see it."

Noah went and got the arrow bringing it to Randolph Grant. He knew right off the arrow was Guardian, but not to whom it belongs. Noah asked "Randolph Grant have you seen this type of arrow before? Do you know whose it is?"

"I do not know who it belongs to, but I know whose kind it belongs to?"

"Who?" Said Noah.

"It would seem to be a Guardian arrow, unless it's not authentic."

"Michael, there is a young girl named Bethany who is an artist. Would you allow for her to draw every aspect of the arrow privately?"

"For what reason?"

"To show it to those on the Island of Reconciliation to see if anyone knows whose it is?"

"I will have her brought to the Grant Manor to draw it in secret."

"Let's us move onto the history of Bennet Grant." Said, Randolph Grant.

BENNET GRANT HISTORY

"The Castellan Army was ecstatic with their victory by deceit. Bennet, now the Grant, surprised them with an attack chasing them off the Island of Reconciliation and kept them off the islands where they retreated to the forest. Bennet found the writings of Ranulf, reports of actions, visitor logs, the plans for the Island of Reconciliation, and the islands of Redemption. He also heard the whispers of those who question whether he was actually chosen as the successor of Ranulf."

"Well, we have a pretty good idea on that one." Said Randolph Grant.

"With suspicion hanging around Bennet Grant and him knowing that he was being watched carefully by the messengers. The changes he made seem to be correct ones. He asked for the Grant Towers to be built to hold the history of the Grants. He said he would select guards to protect the history. However, it was decided that the messengers would protect the history of the Grants and I was asked to select the messengers for each Grant and keep watch over the Grant Towers. He had the Grants Towers built under the palace Treasure Room. There would be one messenger for each Grant that would keep safe all the History of their time.

"Bennet was blessed with wisdom. Bennet would spend a great deal of time in the Study that we are in now praising and praying to ask God for guidance. He always closed the door for privacy during this time.

"The Grant Towers were massive as the messengers not only added the history of the Grants, but of every owner of the Islands, a Map Room was added for every generation, including the history that was known of the Guardians."

"The Grant Towers do not seem to be as big to hold all this history. Where is the rest of the history of the owners, the Guardians and the Map Room located at?" Said, Randolph Grant.

"That is a mystery that we would like to know Randolph Grant as well. It has been hidden and we have tried everything to find it to no avail. Nor do we know why it was hidden or by whom."

"When did it go missing?"

"Soon before Bennet Grant became no more."

"By God's grace we will find it Michael to unlock the mysteries that are hidden in the histories."

"The Castellan was still trying to take the islands for he claimed them all as his. There were constant battles for the lands that visitors to the Island of Reconciliation were turned away and even stopped at one point. This did not go over well for the Island of Reconciliation was a place for those to come to by repentance and faith to reconcile with one another. So, the visitors were allowed to begin coming again and Bennet Grant was tasked with keeping the Islands safe.

"Bennet built his Castle in the Jacob Wall Mountains, where he built a high wall to hold a thousand singers to praise the Lord. He had watched and learned that the Avenskerri would not advance on the island, he placed singers on all the islands that kept the enemy at the Forest of Battleton.

"Bennet had faith and assurance that there was a plan he didn't know what it would be. He knew the Island of

Reconciliation was special for a place for people to reconcile with one another and stand together with their disagreements whatever they were tossed into the sea of forgetfulness by God's loving grace. In the latter years peace was reached for the remainder of time Bennet was the Grant.

"Bennet was going to leave the care of the Island of Reconciliation and all the lands pertaining to it to another person. On faith in a dream, he had of a raven who would reveal his falseness of deceit and deception and would lead them to victory by its death. The one who follow the raven would thrust a true sword of truth given by a Messenger from heaven into the raven of deception. Bennet left the care of the island to Alistair. Which turned out to be a bad decision."

"Games" said Randolph Grant

"What do you mean Randolph Grant?" Said Jacob the messenger for Bennet Grants History.

"It just seems like a game is being played, but for what purpose, that's the question? I have to tell you this is very tiresome. I may need to continue with this tomorrow. We're missing the string that ties everything together."

As he went to get up, he pushed himself away from the table, a part of the table pushed inward, opening a secret compartment underneath the table. They all looked to see if anything was in it and there were missing strings of writings that had been kept hidden in secret all this time.

"What do we have here?" Said Randolph Grant

They investigated the table and found on the left side where the table could also be pushed inward causing another secret compartment to open with more writings.

While everyone was looking at the writings, Mr. Habens was still looking at the table and underneath the table was a lever that he pulled, the top of the table opened. When they lifted up the tabletop, there was the original Will of Ranulf Grant naming Elijah as his successor.

"Michael you will need to get with Gideon and have him remove Bennet and the one he picked to replace Alistair from the Gatehouse of Gideon under suspicion. Have all the messengers in the Grant Towers join us to look over every writing to find the strings to tie all this together."

"Michael called for Arabella informing her to have all the messengers to go over all the writings that have been found and he would be back after visiting Gideon."

"Mr. Habens, you did good!" Said Randolph Grant.

"The Will named Elijah Everard as the successor to Ranulf Grant. There was also a stipulation in the will because he did not want the Island of Reconciliation left to family members or staff unless they met the stipulation. Whoever would succeed a Grant had to be someone whose Lord was Jesus the Christ the Son of the Living God, for God would know the plan and actions needed to keep the island out of the hands of the Avenskerri who are from the Island of Deception."

"Arabella, we need to send a messenger to bring Elijah to the palace."

"I will see to it that it's done."

"Has David the eagle and the messenger sent to Thaddeus Grant returned yet?"

"Not yet sir," said Arabella

"Once they return, we will need to send another message to Thaddeus Grant advising him of what has been found to wait his instructions."

"I will make sure that it is taken care of Randolph Grant." Said Arabella.

"Let's see what treasure of hidden information we have found Mr. Habens. Everything that came out of each of the compartments keep them separate to be looked at. There also seems to be more in the top of the tables hidden compartment as well."

As they began separating and looking at the writings. Quite a lot of the writings were addressed to Banitai from different individuals such as Craveranti and Caselton. Other names in the writings mention Traffanti (the name engraved on Ranulf Everard Mountain Castle), Ravana, Argrannelious, there was a planet alignment of worlds, Lanitani, Daivanti, Chargorikan, Jagoraldine, Pertinia, Guardinia, and Fairalightinia."

"Mr. Habens I will need for you to spend time going over all this information found, to find what game is being played, who is part of the game, the leaders, their purpose, etc. Use the resource of the messengers. Reuben you and I will have to find another room to go over the history of Alistair while they are gleaming through the writings, when done, you can rejoin them."

"Yes sir, there is another room down the hallway." Said Reuben.

172

ALISTAIR GRANT HISTORY

"Alistair saw the peace on the islands and was deceived (so it would seem) by the false messenger that the Avenskerri hadn't tried to attack in years and had abandoned their attempts to take the islands. He removed the singers from the Islands of Redemption and brought them to the Island of Reconciliation.

"The Castellan moved in and took the islands. Alistair immediately knew he had fallen to ill advice and had the singers begin singing praises which stopped their advance. The damage had already been done, allowing the Avenskerri to control the Islands of Redemption.

"Over time, we have learned that there are three Castellan, and we believe they are the same that attacked Ranulf Grant, each has their duties. The three are the Castellan, the Deceiver, and the Disruptor.

1.Castellan is in control of the Military, the garrison, protective of the castle and all its surrounding lands.

2.Deceiver: is the false messenger who lies with deceit and deception

3.Disruptor: is in control of causing uproars, problems outside the Castle. In the communities, villages, the areas away from the castle. The Castellan after taking control of the Islands of Redemption put a barrier up so that no one could come to or from the islands.

"Alistair Grant then began building the high walls on his Castle for the singers to sing day and night. Once finished he had the first group of singers to praise the Lord which kept the Avenskerri from advancing onto the Island of Reconciliation.

"His pride (so it would seem) got in the way he wanted to defeat them because they had tricked him, so he gathered more singers but not the number that was in the plan and spread them out on the high walls and had the singers begin to sing, the barrier weakened two of their guards fell to the ground. The barrier had never weekend before when a greater number of singers were praising only now when there were fewer."

"This dude is in cahoots with the Castellan and Bennet selected him as the Grant? Hopefully, the writings that have been found that were hidden is going to shed the light of truth upon all of this."

"He was the second Castellan of the three, the Deceiver known as the false messenger. Later in the history he will be removed leaving only two." Said Reuben.

"Alistair sent a boat to bring back the two guards with whom he began to pray with. He was alerted that the Avenskerri were advancing, so he had all the singers and his guards to sing praises and the barrier regain its strength, closing so no one could come or go across to the islands, and we believe that is when the other two Castellan came through joining the deceiver Alistair."

"Most likely they were the ones he was supposedly praying with from the boat." Said Randolph Grant. "There have also been sightings of the Avenskerri Armies in the castles of Bennet and Alistair."

"Makes sense that they would be in those castles. Those castles will need to be destroyed. Were their castles also already built into the mountains or did they have them built?"

"Bennet and Alistair had their castles built in those locations."

"There had to be a reason why they built them in those two locations then."

The Successor to Alistair Arrives

"A new group had arrived at Harborshire that would come to the Island of Reconciliation in that group were Thaddeus Frost and Benjamin Everard. Thaddeus Frost was only nine years old, and Benjamin Everard was a couple of years older and made sure no one pick on him. We were excited with joy when we heard that someone from the lineage of Ranulf Grant was on the island. But Benjamin was not selected as the new Grant instead Alistair selected Thaddeus.

"Alistair had watched three people to select from Thaddeus, Benjamin, and a younger man name Caselton who he was ready to select."

Until Mr. Habens said in front of others that he could not find him on the visitor logs.

Caselton was brought to Alistair and was asked, "Where did you come from?"

He lied and said, "I had stowed away on the ship that brought everyone here."

Mr. Habens said, "That is not possible. There are no ships that come to Harborshire. There is only one way to Harborshire and then another way to the Island of Reconciliation. You either have or don't have the ways and if you don't have the ways then you cannot come to either place. What are the ways? If you do not know then you did not come by either way."

Randolph Grant began laughing. "I love Mr. Habens. Most likely Wilford wanted him off the Island of Reconciliation, because of him, calling him out for lying."

"I would say you are correct Randolph Grant." Said Reuben.

"Caselton was sent away but not sent back to the world. Alistair chose Thaddeus Grant as the one who would succeed him while he was dying from being poisoned (we do believe he was poison as he claimed). A note had been found written that said to choose Thaddeus he was younger and weak. We don't know who wrote the note or who advise Alistair to choose Thaddeus to become the Grant."

Randolph Grant asked, "Do you still have the note?"

Reuben replied, "Yes, I'll will go get it for you."

Reuben brought the note back giving it to him. Randolph Grant took the note and began studying the handwriting so if he was to see it again it would solve a mystery of who chose Thaddeus to be the Grant.

"Are you familiar with the handwriting Reuben? What I mean is if you were to see it again would you recognize it?"

"Yes, I believe so."

"Why don't you join the other messengers in the other room reviewing the writings with Mr. Habens and if you come across who you believe it belongs to let me know? Could you also ask the messenger Hope to see me now to go over Kingston Grant's history?"

"Yes sir, I'll send her in."

Kingston Grant History

"The messenger, Hope, came into the room to go over the history of Kingston Grant advising Randolph Grant. "There was not that much history regarding him."

"Let's see what you have."

"Bennet Grant selected David Kingston to replace Alistair as the Grant after Thaddeus Grant learned that Alistair was one of the three Castellan from the Island of Deception. "

Kingston Grants history.

"While not selected to care and protect as the Grant of the Island of Reconciliation his history of care and protection on the Everard Mountain was shown many times in the protection of those who lived there in secrecy."

"Alistair never led an army out of the castle of the Gatehouse of Gideon. Kingston Grant led the armies of angels (messengers) whenever the trumpet was blown by Gideon."

"That's it?" Said Randolph Grant.

"Yes sir," said Hope.

"Tell me of an instance involving his protection of those who lived there."

"The most notable one would be where he protected Dr. Dumpling and Randy. Of course, that was not the name of Dr. Dumpling then, it was Kathryn Everard.

"Really? Hmm...didn't know that? Go on tell me about it."

"Katherinna and Max Everard had seen some beautiful flowers in the meadow. They went to see them while Kathryn carried Randy. Katherinna was Kathryn's aunt, Randy was her son, and she was also a Guardian by the name of Warrior Queen Katherinna. She had agreed to become Max Everard wife for protection and David Kingston was very close to her. They were attacked by the Avenskerri. Katherinna yelled to Kathryn to protect her son, she ran back to the safety of the Everard Mountains calling for help. David Kingston charged the Avenskerri to protect them. Unfortunately, Katherinna and Max Everard were no more. Kathryn raised Randy as her own.

"Was David Kingston a guardian?"

"David Kingston – Selected as a Grant by Bennet Grant. Who is known as Kingston Grant Whose real name is Prince Warrior Kingston. Who had a great love for Warrior Queen Katherinna and close friend to Prince Warrior Bolgerand."

"Doesn't make sense? How was he allowed to keep any part of his Guardian name, when everyone else other than the so call leaders who secured an agreement with Ranulf were not allowed to. Why would he be allowed to unless he was part of the leadership in some way. Who is Prince Warrior Bolgerand? You stated also that Kingston Grant had a great love for Queen Warrior Katherinna, was this love, a love of respect, or some other type of love?"

"Who was this, Bennet?"

"I don't know. These are all good questions that you have and insights. I will need to ask Michael and hopefully he can provide clarity to all of them. I am sorry I am unable to help you with your questions Randolph Grant."

"Hope, you are fine, I just have a lot of questions and suspicions. Wait for Michael's return, until then why don't you go rejoined the other messengers reviewing all the writings."

"Yes sir, thank you for your understanding."

Randolph Grant and Hope walked into the room with all the writings. The messengers and Mr. Habens were scouring through.

Joseph the messenger asked, "Are you ready for me to now to go over Thaddeus Grant's history?"

Randolph Grant said "Yes, just wanted to find out if we're making any head way with the writings?

Mr. Habens said, "What is head way?"

Smiling at Mr. Habens, he said, "It is a figure of speech to see if you have been able to find anything that could solve the mystery."

"OH"

Mr. Habens said, "Randolph Grant, you are going to have to teach me these figures of speech."

"Ok, I can do that. Joseph are you ready?"

"Yes sir," Said Joseph

Thaddeus Grant History

Joseph began to tell of the history of Thaddeus Grant and said although Thaddeus has not been in the Grant Towers, he would not be the only one who hasn't we still have a record of his history on the Island of Reconciliation.

Randolph Grant asked, "Which Grants haven't been in the Grant Towers?"

Joseph replied, "Ranulf Grant who passed on, Alistair has never been in the Grant Towers, and Thaddeus Grant. He then said, "I understand why Ranulf wouldn't have ever been here, and I am sure you are going to explain to me why Thaddeus hasn't been, but why wasn't Alistair ever here when he was the Grant? Before Bennet passed on, he asked that he not be told about the Grant Towers but to keep his history and if able to have Mr. Habens be his historian so that we could obtain his writings, visitor logs, and reports of action. Bennet said that he could not put his finger on what it was, but something wasn't right. Keep the islands safe until the next three Grants arrive together."

Randolph Grant said, "More questions?"

Joseph asked, "What are your questions Randolph Grant, and I will try to answer them for you."

"The questions at this time don't matter." Said Randolph Grant.

"Alistair was never told about the Grant Towers. Be of good cheer Randolph Grant we are being blessed because you are just like Thaddeus Grant."

"Thank you for the compliment." Said Randolph Grant.
Joseph looked at Randolph Grant and smiled.

"Bennet Grant believed by faith that a plan was put in motion, and we are witnessing some steps in the plan although we do not know what the outcome will be. There are going to be three Grants at one time Thaddeus, You, and Evan Randolph."

"How would he know? Did he also say that it would be Thaddeus, Randolph, and Evan Randolph?"

"No, he worded in this way. Wisdom, Protector, and Faithfulness would represent the three Grants that would arrive during a time of turmoil to secure the safety of the Island of Reconciliation and all the lands pertaining to them."

"Mr. Habens was suggested by him to be the historian for Alistair because he had his suspicions of him, and he played his part to get on his good side. He gave all his writings to Thaddeus Grant.

"What is Thaddeus Grant's history, Joseph?"

"Thaddeus Grant met with Mr. Habens and Benjamin he shared everything about Alistair Grant and how there was peace on the islands until Alistair began dismantling all the safety that had been put in place by Bennet."

Michael entered the room. "Be of Good Cheer, Randolph Grant."

"Were you able to take care of the matter with Gideon?"

"Gideon is not going to remove either of them yet from the gatehouse. They will remain sleeping, he would like to let it play out more so instead of removing them on suspicion, to removed them on facts of treason against the Grants."

"Makes sense, as long as I don't have to use them for anything."

"Should anything arise for the need of Gideon's trumpet to blow it has already been decided that I will lead a gatehouse and Ashlyn the messenger to the Guardians would lead the other or a gatehouse of the Guardians messengers."

"Good. Said Randolph Grant. Have you heard anything from David the eagle and Luke the messenger? I thought they would have arrived back by now."

"They have not returned yet. I will send a messenger to check on their whereabouts, we have messengers in the area."

"Thaddeus Grant and I have spoken many times, and he is one with a courageous heart and Love for Jesus the Christ the Son of the Living God and so is the same for Benjamin. Thaddeus decided it was time to put our own trapped into play one that they wouldn't see coming until it was too late. Thaddeus Grant has patience he waited for the answers of prayer to come. He has had his suspicions of Bennet as well, said Michael. He was only nine when he came to the Island of Reconciliation, just a boy, and Benjamin was only eleven between the two of them they found out whom they could trust and who they couldn't trust. Alistair Grant while he was dying on his bed told Thaddeus that he would be the new Grant and that he had been deceived by those on the island with promises. That he had been poisoned with deceit and deception and not to trust the one who he has been running around with Benjamin, instead run with Caselton he is much wiser. Thaddeus was then announced by Alistair as the new Grant. Thaddeus helped him back to his bed and informed him that Benjamin is my friend, he is true and Loves the Lord Jesus with all his heart and soul, and you should be ashamed for lying about his character. Your Caselton I know exactly who he is, he is someone not to trust, I've seen his character too. He then pulled his sword that we had given him and thrust it into Alistair who disintegrated and became a vapor in the wind and blew away. We believe Alistair was the raven (the Castellan Deceiver) in Bennet Grant's dream."

"I am wondering Michael if he actually had a dream or if it was just another deception in the game being played. The history regarding Bennet that was shared with me was *"On faith in a dream, he had of a raven who would reveal his falseness of deceit and deception and would lead them to victory by its death."* If, I am right and this is all a game being played for a plot to take the Island of Reconciliation and all lands pertaining to them, that victory may not represent a victorious win for the Grants, but for whoever is behind this plot to steal something that doesn't belong to them."

"You could be very will correct in your assumption of what is taking place. For there is a devious plot unfolding a little bit at a time. Thaddeus Grant chose wisely for his successor."

"After Thaddeus Grant removed one of the Castellan. That is when Bennet selected David Kingston as the new Grant with the name of Kingston Grant."

"So, question? Ranulf Grant has to know that something is wrong because Elijah is who he selected as his successor, but Bennet is in the Gatehouse of Gideon."

"Ranulf told, Gideon that he didn't select Bennet he selected Elijah. Before Gideon could say anything to him about it, Ranulf stormed off saying his brother is paying him back for all the times he wouldn't listen to him and now he doesn't listen to me. He then slammed the gate to his Castle. He won't talk to anyone about it."

"Michael, was the history of Ranulf written by his account or the account of what the messengers seen or perceived to have seen?"

"It was written on what was seen by the messengers it is accurate."

"Wouldn't it be nice to have Ranulf version of the events? Sometimes what one sees or perceives from actions of others is not the whole story of an event."

"Well let's get back to the history of Thaddeus Grant." Said, Randolph Grant.

"Once Thaddeus was selected and named the Grant. There were two families starting an uproar within the palace community. When it was announced that Alistair was no more the two families began demanding things."

"Kind of sounds familiar, doesn't it?" Said, Randolph Grant.

"There was no record of Brackenshens or Teetson Family anywhere in the visitor logs, so they knew something wasn't right because these families came demanding the Island was theirs, the palace was theirs, everything associated with the island was theirs. In Alistair's notes, he said they were distant family. But there was no record of them, so it was a lie. Horace Brackenshens began dictating what was going to be done and where his families would be living and what their duties would be."

Thaddeus Grant said, "no! I will be selecting whom I want in the positions you have mentioned, and it will not be from any in your families. He then asked Benjamin if he would like to be his Butler and bodyguard?"

Benjamin said, "he would agree to be his butler and bodyguard."

"Horace charged Thaddeus and Benjamin threw him to the ground informing him if he tried it again it would be harder the next time, he hit the ground. When Thaddeus and Benjamin turned to go into the palace."

Horace then again demanded to have their answers for their claim of the islands.

Thaddeus said, "I will pray and give you my decision in the morning."

Then he and Benjamin went into the palace. Horace then followed them in uninvited and Benjamin tossed him out the door. He told him very firmly "If you come back in uninvited again you will not like the end result any better than you do now."

Thaddeus then selected his staff from those he and Benjamin trusted together. If either of them had a question regarding someone picked, they would praise the Lord and pray together asking for God's guidance on the selection. Benjamin would call all those that Thaddeus would select for each duty when he would go out the Brackenshens and Teetsons were still standing waiting for their answer.

He told Thaddeus "They are still standing out there."

Thaddeus said, "Bring Caselton in next."

Benjamin said, "WHY? He is not a good one Thaddeus,"

To which Thaddeus replied, "Yes, I know. I have a plan to put it into action I'll need for him and them to be gone in the morning."

"He told Benjamin his plan and Benjamin smiled and went and got Caselton bringing him to the palace. Thaddeus changed his name to Wilford which Caselton didn't like but went along with it, he had what he wanted to be in the palace where he could devise his attack. Wilford fell asleep and Benjamin kept his eye on him while Thaddeus put his plan in motion. When Wilford awoke in the morning Thaddeus gave him a scroll of parchment rolled up that he had written on for the answer for the Brackenshens and Teetsons families and told him and Benjamin along with some palace guards to take them to the pier and for Wilford to read my answer to them."

"While they were gone, he asked, me if there was someplace that the palace Guards of Bennet and their families could be kept safe along with his family, his brothers and cousins that had come later to Harborshire?"

"I advised him that there was a place, and they would be kept safe by the Messengers Guards. Wilford and Benjamin took the Brackenshens and Teetsons to the pier and Wilford unroll the parchment, and he didn't like at all what was written on it. So much that he asked Benjamin if he would like to read it. Benjamin said, very firmly, 'Thaddeus Grant gave it to you to read to them.'"

Wilford then read what Thaddeus Grant had decreed to them for their answer.

"Horace Brackenshens is a billowing windbag of trouble and I will not stand for his lies or his frivolous demands for his family and the Teetsons, the boat of faith will be arriving soon get on it and get off my island, of course, you'll have to have faith to ride the boat of faith, or you will be swimming to land other than the land you're standing on, or you can have a manor built for you in the Forest of Battleton, of course, you'll have to swim there as well maybe the Avenskerri will let you go through their barrier. My guess is you would rather stay on my island? The deal is this I will build you a manor for the Brackenshens and Teetsons to live in away from the palace and the village and there will be no more lies coming from your mouths, or you will be swimming. Now you can sit there until I figure out where to put your manor."

Thora Teetson asked for a separate manor from the Brackenshens.

Wilford said he would talk to Thaddeus Grant to see if that could be done.

Benjamin said, "I can tell you now the answer is no!"

"Thaddeus Grant built them a manor in the forest of Wary Mist after checking with his friend Silas where would be a good forest for them away from the animals. The remnant of Bennet Grant palace guards and Thaddeus Grant families are being kept safe in Thaddeus Grant's castles within the Courageous Mountains."

"Kathryn is Randy's aunt who is also his protector and mother. She became his mother when Randy's parents Katherinna and her husband wandered outside the Everard Mountains when they saw some beautiful flowers in the meadow. Kathryn your friend was with them carrying Randy."

The Avenskerri attacked them, Randy's parents told, young Kathryn to run with their son to safety. When she reached the safety of the Everard Mountains she called for help. David Kingston and the Messenger Guards fought them off killing them, but Katherinna and Max were no more."

"Kathryn became his mother and protector along with two of Arabella Messenger Guards Josephine and Brooke wherever he goes they are there with him."

"Ok, so Hope had shared this with me when going over Kingston Grants history. I had some questions she could not answer."

"What were your questions, Randolph Grant? I will see if I am able to answer them for you." Said Michael.

"This is what I asked and what Hope had said."

"Was David Kingston a Guardian?"

David Kingston – Selected as a Grant by Bennet Grant. Who is known as Kingston Grant Whose real name is Prince Warrior

Kingston. Who had a great love for Warrior Queen Katherinna and close friend to Prince Warrior Bolgerand.

"Doesn't make sense? How was he allowed to keep any part of his guardian name, when everyone else other than the so call leaders who secured an agreement with Ranulf were not allowed to. Why would he be allowed to unless he was part of the leadership in some way. Who is Prince Warrior Bolgerand? You stated also that Kingston Grant had a great love for Warrior Queen Katherinna, was this love, a love of respect, or some other type of love?"

"Who was this, Bennet?"

"You do know that you are just like Thaddeus Grant in regard to your questioning details? This is why Thaddeus Grant has suspicions regarding Bennet Grant and who he actually was?"

"Thanks for the compliment." Said Randolph Grant.

"It is believed he was a Guardian but has not been able to be confirmed."

"Did you ask any of the Guardians that are here on the Island of Reconciliation?"

"No." Said Michael. "I am the Blessed Messenger of the Grant Manor. Questioning Guardians is not something I am allowed to do. My duty is to the Grants."

"Why?" Said Randolph Grant

"It is complicated, for one he had claimed he was a close friend to Prince Warrior Bolgerand this cannot be confirmed either. It is believed that Prince Warrior Bolgerand is no more."

"Who is he?"

"He is the mate of Warrior Queen Katherinna. It is believed that Kingston Grant's love for the Queen goes much deeper than respect."

You said earlier that it was decided that if needed an Ashlyn who is the Guardians Messenger would lead a Grant's Army instead of Bennet or Kingston. Can she ask for a confirmation on the information?"

"She would require why we are inquiring about a Guardian?"

"So!" Said Randolph Grant.

"I will need to check to see if I am able to talk to her about this situation."

"During this time Thaddeus with praise and prayer asked me if a Bridge of Reconciliation could be built to go from Harborshire to the Island of Reconciliation and then to the Islands of Redemption and onto the Forest of Battleton with only one way to get on the bridge to cross it. There must be true Faith in the Lord Jesus the Christ the Son of the Living God and the bridge could not be seen without faith."

"The Bridge of Reconciliation was built to replace the boat of faith."

"Elijah, a Pastor, learned of the scheme of Wilford to kill Thaddeus, Benjamin, and the fifth Grant. Then replacing them with a child, who Wilford would tell everyone that Thaddeus had chosen him for the next Grant."

"That's why I questioned Bennet Grants raven dream. It's all a scheme, the other shoe just dropped."

"Is that another one of your figures of speech about the shoe dropping?"

Randolph Grant just looked at Michael and smiled.

"The Avenskerri had taken a male child away from her mother on the Island of Redemption to bring to Wilford. They would lay the child on the ground for Wilford. Elijah told Thaddeus of the plot that Wilford was hatching. When the

Avenskerri brought the child through the barrier and laid it on the ground for Wilford to come to get. Elijah switched the boy with Randy. Elijah was a Pastor he was told in a dream who was the mother and where she was, to take the child back to her and preached the Gospel to the Islands of Redemption until the Grant of Grace frees the Islands of Redemption. Elijah and Grace then took the other child with faith walking right through their barrier to find the mother to return her son to her."

"So, Kathryn is family to me?"

Randolph Grant began laughing.

Michael said, "No, she is not an Everard by birth. She is a Guardian and one of the children that were spread throughout the Island by Ranulf."

"Thaddeus was going to choose Benji for the Grant. They both had the same dream that there was a puppy who was being hurt by a pack of wolves and one of their own who had left their pack long ago came to the defense of the puppy and the wolves left because the Wolf didn't back down from all of them, he challenged them all to take a step forward, and they wouldn't like the end result."

"One day Benji told his Uncle Benjamin that he wanted to start helping around the palace asking what he could do. Benjamin said to him, you don't need to do anything wait until you get a bit bigger."

"Mrs. Conogrander, who was Thaddeus Grants cook, called him over in front of Benjamin and said the apple bins are empty get you a wheel barrel to fill it up and take it to the towers by the gate and fill the bins up. She then says to Benjamin you and Thaddeus who is trying to sneak a cinnamon roll can watch to see if he needs any help."

"That is when you showed up and protected Benji. You started to walk away, and Benjamin came and got you and then Thaddeus talked to you, and you said you were sorry for how you treated him. He renamed you, Jackson Randolph."

Randolph Grant began to cry. Isaac who was Randolph Grant's messenger said, "Be of good cheer. Your grandmother Ruth loves you dearly, and she knew from her dream that you were to return to the Island of Reconciliation for that purpose. She and your parents love you greatly and know about all of this. You will see your Grandmother Ruth again one day when you walked through the gates of Heaven."

Randolph Grant said "Thank you, Isaac, for the encouragement. How did the false palace come about?"

Joseph, who was Thaddeus Grant's messenger, said, "Be of good cheer Randolph Grant. Wilford kept talking about the beauty of the Airdrocks Valley and then found what he recalled a record showing where a palace was supposed to have been built in the valley (it was a false record) that had been written by Alistair."

"Thaddeus built the false palace with Wilford thinking he was in control. Thaddeus made sure to have a lot of ways into the palace for when Wilford decides to take control. Here is a map of all the passageways in and around the place."

"Thaddeus asked Kathryn to befriend Albert who she did not like at all because he always picked on a boy, she did like a lot. Thaddeus explain why he needed her to befriend Albert because they knew that was the family Wilford was going to give Randy to. She saw a side that others didn't, there was good in him, and she fell in love with him. They married, and they had that argument that opened the door of opportunity when Wilford brought her to Thaddeus thinking he had the upper hand when he didn't."

"Thaddeus showed him tough love something he had never in his life experienced. Albert was very stubborn he wasn't going to read the Bible that Thaddeus had left him. One day Randy picked up the Bible walked over to Albert and said read Daddy Dumping. Kathryn looked at him with a smile on her face."

Albert said, "I guess you put him up to this?"

Kathryn replied, "She didn't say anything to Randy about having you read his favorite book."

Randy opened the book randomly to the book of Romans Chapter 8 and said, "Read daddy."

Albert looked at where his son wanted him to read, and he began to read. His son crawled into his lap and listened to what was being read and Albert's ears were open, and his heart was softened by the Word of God. He and Kathryn study the Bible together daily while Randy would sit and listen. Wilford came by weekly and couldn't answer their questions and tried to feed them his false beliefs eventually he stopped coming. Kathryn was able to lead Albert to the Lord.

Randolph Grant excused himself. He was going to rest and ponder on everything that had been revealed to him in the towers. "Mr. Habens we'll prepare a room for you in the manor for you to stay in."

Mr. Habens said, "Can I just have a bed brought here I have a lot of catching up to do."

"I don't know how we will get a bed down here without everyone knowing it. But I'll see what can be done."

Michael said, "We can provide for him a room in the towers to sleep in and the comforts he would require Randolph Grant."

Randolph Grant said, "Thank you, Michael, you and all your messengers are a blessing and greatly appreciated. Thank you, Lord Jesus, for providing them for our help. Let me know when David and your messenger arrive back. Arabella has another message to send to Thaddeus Grant when they return with what has been discovered."

"I'll will let you know." Said Michael.

Randolph Grant History

"Thaddeus Grant chose Randolph Grant when he was a very young boy who use to run with the bullies on the Island of Reconciliation who broke away from the pack. He and his family had left the Island of Reconciliation for some time. Thaddeus Grant had a dream one morning of very small puppy who was being attacked by a pack of wolves. A voice out of nowhere said 'leave him alone' and then he awoke from his dream."

"Benji, who was Benjamin's nephew, had come to visit and reconcile with his Uncle Benjamin while on the Island of Reconciliation he also had a dream of a small puppy who had managed to spill some apples on the ground while running after the apples to catch them as they rolled away the puppy was surrounded by a pack of wolves who planned not only to eat the apples but the puppy as they lunged for the puppy he awaken from the dream."

"Randolph's grandmother Ruth had a dream. She told her grandson that he was needed on the Island of Reconciliation that there was a puppy in need of a protector. She believed he was the guardian for the puppy to keep him safe from harm and the two of you would become lifelong friends."

"Benji kept asking his uncle for something to do to help around the palace."

"His Uncle Benjamin said you need not worry about doing anything you are here as a guest and besides wait until you grow more.

"Benji was very small for his size, and he became dejected."

"Mrs. Conogrander had heard everything."

"She told Benji she could use some help if he would like to help her?"

"Benji eyes lit up with joy."

"While Benjamin and Thaddeus just stared at Mrs. Conogrander."

"She told them they could watch from the doorway should he need any help. Mrs. Conogrander said the apple bins need to be filled so all those on the Island of Reconciliation could help themselves to them because they were free."

"Benji not thinking of his dream at all loaded the wheelbarrow with apples and did his best to roll it towards the towers at the entranceway, all the while Benjamin and Thaddeus would watch grinning as he pushed the wheelbarrow. When he got them to the empty bins, he opened the lid. He did his best to lift the wheelbarrow up so the apples would pour into the bins. Some did and quite a few miss the bins altogether rolling out onto street. He went to pick up the apples when he was surrounded by the bullies in the neighborhood who began harassing him, pushing him, and bullying him for his size. They knock him to the ground a few times and Benji became scared looking around for help they were all much bigger than him."

"He prayed for help. As the bullies were moving closer to him. A voice out of nowhere said, 'LEAVE HIM ALONE!'"

"They all turned to see who told them to leave him alone. Once they knew who it was, they began to walk away. One said that they would see you later munchkin. The voice said, 'no you won't.' They all turned around. He said to them if anyone of you takes a step towards him, I'll defend him, if you take a step to the right or the left, I'll defend him, the only step you have is backwards. Now get out of here and leave him alone!"

"Thaddeus Grant and Benji both realized that the one who was protecting Benji (the puppy) was the voice in their dream."

"Randolph apologized to Thaddeus for always giving him a hard time and stealing the apples when they could have them for free."

"Thaddeus Grant offered him an apple, but Randolph replied that he didn't really like apples.
Thaddeus Grant said he didn't either, but they had an overabundance of them and had to get rid of them."

"Benji and Randolph became friends. In time Thaddeus Grant chose Randolph to be his successor."

"He had cared and protected a young boy who would become his successor as Grant whose name would be Evan Randolph Grant. Upon learning that one of his young guards John who was only fifteen was cruelly beaten and tormented by the estate guards he then accepted the path chosen for him long ago."

"After being announced he corrected Terry Teetson of the deception and lies that he had been told. He stood on the battlefield against the Estate Guards preaching to them repentance and many were saved while others were sent back into the world. He brought Mr. Habens home."

"He uncovered the secret writings in the Grant Towers hidden in secret compartments in the desk with the Help of Mr. Habens."

"Began improvements for the Grant Palace Estates choosing Jonathan to lead the crews. There would be much more written about the Randolph Grant's History including what would take place in the next few days."

Philip R Evans

Evan Randolph Grant History

"The Evan Randolph Grant History is yet to be written for he has not been announced as of yet. His adventures that await his history will be great. Evan means the Lord is gracious and Randolph means shield wolf."

Thaddeus Grant Captured

It was still evening when Randolph Grant left the Grant Towers walking outside and watching the sky for David and the messenger's return. *Why have they not returned?* He became concerned. He sent a messenger to find Silas, the Red Squirrel, to tell him about his concern for David. The eagle who flew to the palace with a messenger to deliver a message to Thaddeus Grant had not returned. "See if he can find out any information as to why from the other animals?"

Elijah was brought to the Grant Manor to see Randolph Grant and Michael the messenger. When in the study, Elijah was notified that he was chosen by Ranulf to be the Grant to succeed him and not Bennet.

Randolph Grant said, "We found the true Will of Ranulf Grant that had been hidden and that there seemingly is a plot to take the Island of Reconciliation that you apparently are aware of."

Elijah said, "I am aware. If I can be of assistance to you Randolph Grant or Thaddeus Grant just let me know and I will be of service to you. I do not know how to make the wrong right for what has been taken from you being a Grant."

"There is nothing to make right. I will not challenge for the position of being a Grant. Thaddeus Grant is a man of God with wisdom and courage, and I believe he has chosen wisely of you as his successor. I am just blessed that my brother Ranulf would have thought so highly of me to be his successor. He was a good man. He was treated unfairly by our other half brothers who were full of all kinds of deceit and jealousy towards Ranulf. Did you and he ever talk regarding the wrongs done to the Guardians and a forest?"

Michael just stared at Randolph Grant but said nothing.

Elijah said, "Oh yes, he was so miserable about events that happened at the forest and the guardians blaming him for the castle that was built on the high mountain. I don't know if my brother was hallucinating or not. Elijah was smiling with a laugh. "A little Corilevava came out of the Oak tree, at the top of the mountain, telling him to build the Castle to block the oak tree from seeing the forest. Then the little Corilevava crawled back into the oak tree. So, he did."

"Were there any other conversations with Ranulf Grant regarding the events there?"

Elijah said, "I am a fisher of men. It sounds as though you are fishing for answers Randolph Grant regarding my brother Ranulf."

"To be quite honest with you Elijah, I am trying to understand his choices that he made during that time that would help clarify the events."

"I understand and thank you for being honest Randolph Grant. There was a conversation regarding all the children that were brought to the Island of Reconciliation that were spread across to different parts. This broke his heart for he loves children and I asked why did you do that to them? He said, because their Queen said it would protect them from some of the more mature warriors still on the Islands of Transformation, Strength, and Kindness holding off the enemy. She also said for them to have their names changed so the ones who would hurt them would not know who they were."

Michael asked, "What was the name of this Queen?"

Elijah said, "My brother said he could not remember the name of the Queen only that she was a Warrior Queen. He was afraid what the mature warriors would do to the children, so he had them put in the guardhouse. They vehemently deny that they would hurt the young Guardians."

"I thank you for sharing with us this information. It is late, come we will have a room prepared for you to rest the night before your journey back home."

Randolph Grant looked at Michael and said, "Kind of changes the facts of the history, doesn't it? Anyway, to determine how many Warrior Queens would have been there at the time?"

"Yes, it does." said Michael. "I have no doubt he was telling the truth as well. I have known Elijah for some time, and he has never been dishonest when I spoke with him about matters. We'll have to check the history to see."

"Should David and your messenger arrive wake me, or if Silas should bring information as to why they have not returned as of yet, which concerns me, let me know as well."

"I will Randolph Grant."

The next morning Randolph Grant, after having a dream the night before, decided to lay a trap to see if he could find out who was the author of the note for Thaddeus Grant to succeed Alistair as the Grant of the Island of Reconciliation.

Randolph Grant told, his commander, Jack, "Have everyone in the guardhouse write their names and where they are from on a ledger. if they ask why, say to them: 'You do want out of the guardhouse, don't you?' Take guards with you and make sure each one signs their information and not someone for them. Then bring the ledger to me."

Michael greeted him "Be of good cheer Randolph Grant."

"Hi, Michael. So, what do you have on our plate today?"

Michael replied, "I don't have a plate."

Randolph Grant smiled and said "It was a figure of speech. What do I need to know today?"

Randy came running into the room. "Mr. Grant, I had another dream last night you want to hear it?"

Randolph Grant told Randy "I had one too. What was yours?"

"I had a dream of hands writing on a piece of paper. I couldn't see what they were writing. When they were done, I looked at the paper, and it said, 'younger weakling.' I'm not a weakling."

Randolph Grant said to Randy," No you're not. Greater is He that is in you, than he that is in the world. I had the same dream, and I don't believe the dream is talking about you or me. When I find out who it is I'll let you know ok?"

Randy said, "ok."

Michael said, "Do you know?"

Randolph Grant replied, "We may find out in a bit."

The commander came back in the room with the ledger and handed it to Randolph Grant.

"Michael, could you stay here and if anyone needs me, can you let me know, ok? I am going to visit Mr. Habens for a moment."

Michael said that he could do that.

Randolph Grant went to the Grant Towers. When he saw Mr. Habens, he asked to see the note again recommending Thaddeus Grant for the successor to Alistair Grant. He looked over the names on the ledger and the handwriting on the note matched the handwriting of a name that had been written on the ledger. Randolph Grant rushed back up to where Michael was. "We have a match for the handwritten note. I know who told Alistair to select Thaddeus for the Grant.

Michael said, "Who?"

"Ambrose! I believe he is the disruptor. He took the community farm away from Neville, who pointed him out in Bennet Village where Agar and his crew were. They were causing problems in the village and when I asked him where his home was, he said the Forest of Avenskerri. It didn't ring a bell with me when he said where he was from."

"I take it that's another figure of speech, ringing bells?"
Randolph Grant just looked at Michael smiling.
He then turned to his butler. "Benji"
"Yes sir."
"Tell my commander to bring out Ambrose guarded."
Benji said "I will tell him."
Michael handed Randolph Grant a True Sword of the Grants, and said, "When he sees the sword he will back away with fear. You will need to thrust it into him before he can call on the Avenskerri to come here."

Ambrose was brought out of the guardhouse. He thanked Randolph for his release.

Randolph Grant said, "I read your note telling Alistair to select Thaddeus Grant as the Grant because you thought he was young and weak. I tell you now when he is at his weakest point, God is at his STRONGEST.

He pulled the sword.

Ambrose backed away with great fear, the guards held him while Randolph Grant thrust the sword into him, he disintegrated like a vapor and the wind blew him away.

The guards that were in the guardhouse came out. One of them said "Agar and the other prisoners that were brought in with him have disappeared."

Randolph Grant asked, "What about Terry and Burt?"
"They're still here. Gunnar led them to the Lord last night."
Randolph Grant said, "Check on Terry and Steven!"

Benji said, "Pastor Dumpling and Kathryn led them both to the Lord. They have been sharing the Gospel with them since they have been back."

Randolph Grant turned to Michael to give him back the sword.

Michael told him the sword was his to keep.

Randolph Grant knelt on the ground and praised the Lord. He asked for wisdom and guidance to restore peace to the Island of Reconciliation and bring freedom to the Islands of Redemption.

Michael knelt beside him placing his hand on his shoulder. "Be of good cheer. Today has brought us another step closer to the plan that has been put in motion to bring peace and freedom. For it is written: 'But my God shall supply all your need according to his riches in glory by Christ Jesus'."

Randolph Grant raised up and saw Randy standing there.

Randy said, "Mr. Grant, was that who the dream was about?"

Randolph Grant went to him and knelt down and said, "Yes."

Randy said, "I don't understand what just happened. Was that a trick?"

Randolph Grant didn't know how to answer him. Then said, "You remember when Silas said hello to you?"

Randy said, "Uh-huh."

Randolph Grant said, "Something like that doesn't happen in the world you were in before you came here, right?"

Randy said, "Uh-huh."

Kathryn then came out of the palace asking, "Is everything alright?" Michael informed her what happened.

She came over to them and said, "I'll explain it to him."

Randolph Grant said, "I didn't know he was there Kathryn." He Looked at her with a dazed stare.

Kathryn said, "It's ok, he follows you everywhere "

Randy said, "I love him mom, he protected and cared for me."

Kathryn said, "What you saw was him protecting everyone on the Island of Reconciliation."

Randy said, "That's what he does."

Kathryn smiled and kissed her son on the cheek. "Let's let Michael and Mr. Grant talk, so they can do some more protecting." She carried him into the manor.

Michael smiled and said, "Be of good cheer Randolph Grant. He will be ok. I came to greet you this morning to say that Thaddeus Grant would be best served back here as the Grant in the rightful palace. We would need his report of actions and visitor logs that he has kept secret from all except Benjamin who is his trusted friend as Benji is to you. Daniel and his officers, the guards who Pastor Dumpling and you led to the Lord and those who are truly in service to Thaddeus Grant, his staff that he chose, and their families need to be brought back as well."

"What of the others that are there?" said Randolph Grant

"All others will need to stand on the field and the armies of the Grants will sweep across the field and all surrounding areas of Airdrocks Valley. Those that remain will return with everyone as well. The others that are removed will be sent back to the world without knowledge of the Island of Reconciliation In hope that they will find repentance and faith in the Lord Jesus the Christ the Son of the Living God."

"When you say the armies of the Grants, you are not talking of sending Bennet and Kingston are you? There is too much suspicion in regard to them."

"No, they will not lead the Grant armies from the Gatehouse of Gideon."

Randolph Grant said, "Undoubtedly, Wilford most likely knows that he doesn't have his ally anymore." He glanced into the sky and with joy and pointed as he saw David the eagle land by him.

"We could not get the message to Thaddeus Grant."

Silas climbed out from his feathers carrying the message that was sent.

Michael asked, "Where is the messenger Luke at? Why could you not deliver the message to Thaddeus Grant?"

David said, "Before we arrived, Alexander the leader of the Grey Wolves, saw a great number of Avenskerri coming through the barrier. He followed them to see where they were going, so he could report it to Thaddeus Grant. They captured the palace in the Airdrocks Valley freeing Wilford from the stocks."

"Why was Wilford in the stocks?"

"The commander, Daniel, caught Wilford trying to poison Thaddeus Grant. Therefore, he was put in the stocks. After Wilford was able to take the palace he placed Thaddeus Grant, the commander, and the manor guards in the stocks. Luke is still at the palace. He was able to remain unseen by Wilford and his

Avenskerri guards. He learned valuable information and relayed it to me to bring back to Randolph Grant and you Michael." said, David the Eagle.

"What has he learned?" said Randolph Grant

Luke said, "Wilford is laughing because he believes you have no clue what you are up against. He has set the plan in motion to reclaim his islands and lands. Just as he foiled the plans of Ranulf Grant he has foiled already your plan of attack against him trying to retake his beautiful palace."

"I don't even know my plan yet. When I do, he won't know what is coming."

"Randolph Grant, what is being said has been confirmed by messengers who we have in the Airdrocks Valley." said Michael.

Blue jays, Archibald, and Maribel. landed and said, "We can't stay. We have to find safety because there are a lot of Ravens flying this way. They are a way back, but there are a lot of them. We saw them in the Airdrocks Valley."

Michael said, "This is not good."

David the eagle who is the commander of all the animals said, "We'll help you. Just tell us what you need, Michael."

"Why is it not good Michael?" Asked Randolph Grant.

"When the Avenskerri first arrived in our world they attacked the Guardians with Ravens. They are not birds. They are like the Castellan who have taken the form of humans, in this case ravens. They will then change to Avenskerri guards once they drop from the sky. This is how they robbed the guardians' children scooping in and taking them.

"Commander, get me Gareth."

"He is in the guardhouse by order of Commander Daniel until he returns."

"Get me Gareth. Who is in charge of the Archers while John is healing? Bring whoever it is to me."

"I will find out while getting Gareth." Answered the commander.

Michael said, "The arrows will not have any effect on them Randolph Grant."

"They will if the arrow heads are the same as the true swords of the Grants and I'll need twenty swords of the Grants for Gareth and his guards that will be going with him for any that land."

"I will be right back with them."

The commander arrived with Gareth and Kaitlyn who oversaw the Archers while John was healing.

"Commander, Gareth, Kaitlyn, come with me, David, Archibald and Maribel come also."

"What about me?" Said, Silas the red squirrel.

Randolph Grant motioned for Silas who jumped into his arms then onto his shoulder. When entering the Grant Manor, Randolph Grant asked Benji to find a safe place for Archibald and Maribel. They went to the Great Hall before he addressed the crowd. "We have some Avenskerri Ravens on the way. Gareth you will have to have a line defense on the ground against them. Kaitlyn, select the most accurate archers you have."

Gareth said, "Our swords and arrows will have no effect against them."

"The swords and arrows I give you to defend our people will. Michael has gone to get your special weapons."

David said, "My eagles can carry the archers of the messenger guard."

Michael returned, "Be of Good Cheer everyone. Gareth these swords are like the True Swords of the Grants, they will destroy the Avenskerri by thrusting it into them. Kaitlyn the arrow tips are also like the Swords of the Grants. David, we accept your offer our archers will fly with you, and we also have something for you that we can put on your talons for your safety.

I would go with you Gareth and Kaitlyn but Thaddeus Grant, Commander Daniel, and the other manor guards at the palace have all been captured. I must come up with plan to rescue all of them."

Kaitlyn said, "I would like to have someone go with us who has experience fighting the Avenskerri firsthand."

"Who?" Asked Randolph Grant.

"The guard, Gunnar, is a Guardian. As am I."

Gareth said, "With Gunnar, none of them will escape for I know him. Matter of fact he will set a defense that they will not see coming."

"Ask him if he will join you." Said, Randolph Grant.

Commander Jack said, "I would like to join them."

"Please understand commander, I will need you here in case any do get through. Michael will provide you with the same weapons."

As they all left. Gareth went to ask Gunnar to join them. The commander sent guards to gather everyone in the Bennet Village and sound the alarm in the village for everyone in the surrounding areas to be brought to the Grant Manor. He asked for volunteers for a mission to destroy Avenskerri Ravens informing them they had the weapons to do it. Kaitlyn chose her most accurate archers, leaving Hunter in charge while she was away. They left to set the surprise. Kathryn was waiting outside the Great Hall for Randolph Grant. Silas was still on Randolph Grant's shoulder.

When he came out. Kathryn said, "Randolph Grant, Randy took a nap and had another dream. This dream had black birds falling out of the sky by the bunches. Some landed that looked like men and then they turned into a black smoke like the one earlier today."

Randolph Grant said, "Avenskerri Ravens are on the way. We have set a surprise for them. Gareth, Gunnar, and Kaitlyn will be meeting them with special weapons to drop them from the sky and destroy them on the ground. Should any get through the commander, Jack, guards at the manor will eliminate the threat with the same weapons.

Michael said, "They will all return safely, winning this battle."

Randolph Grant said, "I'll be back shortly, I need to go check for something that Thaddeus Grant mentioned to me once that might help." Before leaving Randolph Grant asked Michael to place messengers to all the entrances into the Grant Manor Estates in case needed. "Kathryn we could use your help. The villagers are being brought to the Grant Manor; they can go to the under-croft. There is plenty of room there to hold everyone.

The staff and guest in the manor will be going there as well. That would include the guest on my shoulder.

Silas took a stare at Randolph Grant.

"Randy will be in the under-croft he'll need your protection."

"Yes sir, I will protect him." Said Silas.

He left everyone to go to the Treasure Room remembering *when Thaddeus Grant first showed me the treasure room, the table that had Thaddeus Grant's most precious gem on it. There was compartment that had a lever in it that would provide the answer to questions I would need when the time came. All I have to do is ask the question that I don't have an answer for.* He stood there looking at the table. He firmly asked, "Is there a plan in place to free those in captivity from the false palace, bring freedom and peace to the Islands of Redemption and the Islands of Reconciliation, breaking the barrier, destroying the false palace, and removing the Avenskerri from the Island of Reconciliation?"

The compartment opened with a lever, he pulled the lever, a new room in the Treasure Room opened behind him.

THE BATTLE FOR PEACE AND FREEDOM

$\mathcal{R}$andolph entered the room. There was a table with a book sitting in the center and it was very dusty, which didn't make sense for no rooms were ever dusty. While looking over the book, he smiled, shook his head, then said, "You're so predictable, you think your wise and you are dumber than a doorknob."

"Be of Good Cheer, Randolph Grant. Is that another figure of speech as well?"

"Yes, it is, Michael."

I thought this might be where you were heading. Thaddeus Grant had said, 'If the time comes where this situation arises, you are to follow Randolph Grant for the plan that has been given to me.' Thaddeus Grant praised the Lord morning, day, and night seeking for guidance and wisdom for he knew this day would come. So, what is dumber than a doorknob?"

"I don't think Wilford is as strong without his other two counterparts that have been eliminated by the True Swords of the Grants. He makes more mistakes, for without the others, deceitful parts they play, he is left on his own to play their parts. He has always been overconfident, even more so now that he is by himself leaning on his own understanding."

"What you say regarding Wilford, I would say you are correct. However, he is the Castellan that, as you say, plays the part, which is the military. So be careful and wise in your decisions going forward against him. Do not underestimate him, for he did send the ravens to attack the Grant Manor; something we were not expecting."

"Once again Michael, you have brought wisdom to our conversation which I thank you for." He then shared with Michael what he had asked when in the Treasure Room. "The compartment opened with a lever, I pulled it and this room opened. Do you notice anything about the book on the table?"

"It's very dusty."

"Anything else? Take a really good look at it."

"He must really like that design." Said, Michael, "What are you going to do with it?"

Randolph Grant stepped out of the room and Michael did as well. The door to the room closed. He went to his knees in prayer asking, "Father in heaven, I have no doubt you gave Thaddeus Grant a plan of action for this time that we are in. I fear it is lost by the hands of the enemy. Show us the way and keep our guards safe as they go into battle against the enemy. In Jesus name."

Michael was kneeling beside Randolph Grant, in agreement with his prayer. They waited as Thaddeus Grant would have done. They both heard a small still voice within them. *Ask, and it shall be given you; seek, and ye shall find; knock, and it shall be opened unto you: For everyone that asketh receiveth; and he that seeketh findeth; and to him that knocketh it shall be opened.* They shared with one another what had been heard. Randolph Grant stood up asking again with a variation on what he had asked before.

"Is the plan that was given to Thaddeus Grant to free those in captivity at the false palace, from Wilford the Castellan of the Avenskerri, to bring freedom and peace to the Islands of Redemption and the Islands of Reconciliation? Also, to break thru the barrier, destroy the false palace, remove the Avenskerri and the Castellan from the Island of Reconciliation?"

The compartment opened again, and he pulled the lever. The door behind him opened and the table was still in the room, with the same book atop it. There was, however, one change; Ranulf Grant was standing there.

"I am here to give you Thaddeus Grant's plan that was given to him. Randolph Grant, you kick this Castellan off our Island of Reconciliation. Michael, I hope when this is done you will visit with me at my Castle at the Gatehouse of Gideon. Thaddeus Grant has seen the plan of Wilford and suggested you use it against him. Implement the plan also given to Thaddeus Grant by prayer."

"Do you have to leave now?" Said Randolph Grant.

"No, if you would like I can stay until Gideon calls me back to the Gatehouse. There is one thing though, I did not select Bennet as the Grant and you should not trust him or the other

215

one. He has chosen to replace him whose name I am not even going to waste my breath mentioning."

Michael said, "We found your true Will selecting Elijah as your successor. He is here in the manor if you would like to see and talk with him. I can arrange it."

"I would like that greatly. Michael. You will put it in the record of my history that I claim Elijah as my brother?"

"Yes, it will be done."

Michael sent a messenger asking that Elijah be brought to the Treasure Room. Elijah was ecstatic upon seeing Ranulf and being able to talk to him.

"I don't want to interrupt your reunion, but we need to see Thaddeus Grant's plan." Said Randolph Grant.

Ranulf Grant said, "You will need the following people: Michael, Benji, Kathryn, Pastor Dumpling, Randy, his guards Samuel, Severin, William, James, your commander Jack, the guard with the greatest faith to break the barrier, and Mr. Habens.

He wrote the names down. Upon leaving the room, he gave the note to Benji instructing him to bring everyone including himself to the Treasure Room and he would be there waiting for them. Benji gathered all of them except the commander Jack who had his guards watching for any Avenskerri who might escape the surprise. Silas came along on Randy's shoulder.

Silas said, "I am protecting still."

"We will need to wait for my commander to return and Gunnar. Michael, can you see how it's going with the battle if need be. Saddle me a horse and I will join them.

I will see and return shortly."

They waited to hear from Michael.

"Elijah, please tell the guardian children in the room that I am sorry." Tears fell from his eyes. In time, the history will show that not all that I did was done by my choice but by others of their kind who deceived me."

Kathryn said, "We can see and hear you Ranulf Grant and I believe what you have said here and forgive you, even for the things that were your own doing.

All the Guardians in the room told him they too forgave him and believed what he has said, and that time will tell the truth.

"Thank you all." Said Ranulf Grant.

Michael returned within the hour, "Be of Good Cheer, everyone, the battle has been won.
No one escaped and the guards are returning safely. Gunnar and the commander have been informed that they are needed here now."

Randolph Grant continued to stare at the book on the table. When a black cloud rose up from inside. It stood tall amongst everyone.

Then a voice said, "You cannot defeat the Avenskerri. Your weapons are useless against my armies that will arrive shortly and take your children for our armies. We will take back our Islands and lands and destroy all of you and the guardians who stand with you against me."

Randolph Grant said, "Everyone out of the room now."

"It will do no good to send them to hide. My armies will find them."

As they all began to leave the room Michael saw the commander and Gunnar enter the Treasure Room. Both carrying the True Swords of the Grants with them.

"Hurry into the room before the door is shut." Said Michael.

They entered the room seeing the large black cloud that was still boasting of its victory to come by its armies that would arrive shortly.

Randolph Grant said, "Your armies are no more."

Ranulf Grant was the first to thrust his sword into the black cloud, followed by Randolph Grant and joined by Gunnar and the commander. Then they all raised their swords bringing them down hard and swift on the Black Cloud and book. It disintegrated into dust on the floor.

Michael appeared, "Be of good cheer. Everyone, the threat has been eliminated."

Randolph Grant said, "We need to have this dust cleaned up. Shame we can't drop it on Wilford's head."

"I can arrange for it to happen Randolph Grant." Said Michael.

"Do it."

Meanwhile, back at the false palace where Wilford had been listening to everything going on in the room at the Grant Manor through the book in the real palace. His book exploded sending him slamming against the wall as the black cloud became a vapor blown away by the wind.

Thaddeus Grant and the others, in the stocks at the time, saw the black vapor being blown away from the false palace.

Smiling and shaking his head Thaddeus said, "Wilford has no idea who he is up against."

They all laughed.

Wilford walked out of the false palace standing and staring with a smirky grin at them in the stocks. Dust fell from the sky covering him. They all began to laugh uncontrollable. Wilford wiped the dust from him as it was being blown away by a gust of wind. He then stomped back into the false palace.

Back at the Grant Manor, Ranulf Grant said to the door, "Show Randolph Grant the plan that was given to Thaddeus Grant and the names he has chosen for this task at hand."

Thaddeus Grant's handwriting appeared, writing the plan, "Trust in the LORD with all your heart; do not depend on your own understanding. Seek his will in all you do, and he will show you which path to take." Proverbs 3:5-6 NLT

Randolph Grant gathered with everyone who played a vital role in the rescue operation they all knelt in a circle, holding hands. With one voice of unity, they praised God. Each one lifted prayer for wisdom, guidance, and protection for the plan to be successful for God's Glory.

Thaddeus Grant's handwriting appeared again after they had prayed. "Most of the time when having an opponent one will look for the weakest in their attack even exploiting it will still leave them with their strength to attack from. If, however you can make their strength weak, then all they can do is fall back to their weakness in their attack. Find the strength, weaken it, and then win."

"What is his strength?"

Randolph Grant said, "Over confidence. Being sure of himself and thinking he has an upper hand. I think the biggest advantage he thinks he has will come from the Grant's armies being led by Bennet and Kingston.

"Have each one read their part in the plan. Choose the guard with the most faith to break the barrier. Pray for wisdom, guidance, and success. If I am not there with you, then something must have happened. I chose you for my successor for a reason and I have no doubt the enemy underestimates your ability, but I don't. Go spank him good."

They each spent the rest of the day studying the plan and their role for it to be a success. Randolph Grant with Michael's help made a few changes. Randolph Grant wanted to make sure everyone knew their role, so he called upon each individual or group to review their part.

He first asked Mr. Habens and Gunnar to come see him.

Randolph Grant said to his guard Gunnar, "I chose you because I believe that you have the strongest faith for the task of breaking the barrier that is between the Island of Reconciliation and the Islands of Redemption. Mr. Habens will give a note to Gideon"

Gunnar said, "All things are possible with God. The faith of a mustard seed can move mountains. a barrier is only an obstacle that needs to be moved and by God's Grace it will move out of our way for the Glory of God."

Randolph Grant knew Mr. Habens was nervous and pulled him to his side placing his arm around him and said, "You will have a safe journey and a safe return, you are my historian, and you were chosen for that reason and because Gunnar will need you at the Grant's Castle to inform Bennet and Kingston, we have our suspicions. When Gideon's Trumpet blows Ranulf Grant will lead his armies out of his castle. Gunnar you will ride with Ranulf Grant to a place where you will meet up with another messenger guard led by Ashlyn the messenger of the Guardians. Do not fear Mr. Habens, the Lord will be with you."

Eagles were landing, ready to carry Silas who oversaw the squirrels who would scout ahead for the safest routes to advance on the false palace. Michael had given a special key to an eagle who took flight to fly to the Gatehouse of Gideon with Mr. Habens and Gunnar who had been placed inside the key.

He then called for Kathryn, Pastor Dumpling, Randy, and his personal guards Samuel, Severin, James, William, along with the messenger guard who will lead everyone on the Island of Reconciliation through the secret passageway to Grace Mountain.

Randy said, "Mr. Grant aren't you coming?"

"I will see you later at Grace Mountain."

Randolph Grant called for Michael and said, "Is there no way we can announce him now?"

Michael replied, "Be of good cheer it is not time for him to be announced."

He then said to Michael, "Pastor Dumpling, his dad may not be originally from the Island of Reconciliation, but as you have said he is saved and belongs to the Lord. This makes him a new creature in Christ Jesus."

Michael replied, "Be of good cheer. You are correct in what you say, and it is something that Thaddeus Grant will have to decide on for he is the Grant of the Island of Reconciliation. We must prepare for today the Eagle will be at the Gatehouse of Gideon within a few hours."

Pastor Dumpling had tears in his eyes and came over to Randolph Grant and said, "I was told I wouldn't be allowed to witness his announcement, thank you for trying."

Randolph Grant replied, "I will ask Thaddeus Grant, after he is rescued. Should he say yes, it is not I who you should then thank. The Glory belongs to the Lord. When you accepted Jesus as your personal Lord and Savior you became a new creature in Christ Jesus, the old has been washed away."

Those from the village and surrounding areas were making their way into the secret passage to the tunnel. At the end of the tunnel was a Bridge of Reconciliation that would take them to Grace Mountain safely where they would be met by palace guards from Everard Mountain.

Randolph Grant readied his guard for the ride to the false palace going over the plans with his Commander and his officers. "Once Gunnar completes his task by faith in breaking the barrier, he and the Ashlyn Guardians Army will sweep across the Islands of Redemption freeing them of the Avenskerri. Michael's messenger guards, led by Alyssa, will sweep through the Jacob Wall Mountain Castle and Michael will sweep through Kingston Bliss Mountain Castle removing the Avenskerri. Both of these castles will then be destroyed by Michael's messenger guards.

Ranulf Grant will split his forces. "One will go through the secretive tunnels and sweep the lower levels of the false palace. My friends on Wolf Mountain will introduce themselves to the palace guard at the false palace."

Commander Jack asked, "May we inquire as to who your friends are, sir?"

Randolph Grant smiled then said, "Alexander, Randson, and Snowy, who are the leaders of the gray, red, and arctic wolves. They will gather any guards who are able to escape the palace from the Grant Armies. Ranulf Grant will send his guards through the tunnels leading into the false palace."

Michael brought a special sword to Randolph Grant that would give him an advantage over Wilford. They had discussed it prior.

Randolph Grant and his guard began their march from the Grant Manor in the evening. With his banner colors of blue and gold with a silver R, a gold sword in the middle, below were three wolves together a white, red, and gray.

Those in the village made their way through the secret passageway where many were asking questions as to what was happening? Why there were so many guards? Many wanted to leave the Island of Reconciliation and go to Harborshire.

Pastor Dumpling informed them, "You will be safer here."

Randy asked, "Would you like to hear something I have read that is really neat?"

Some smiled, while others just wanted to find somewhere to hide for fear of the unknown as anxiety began to take its hold on many of them. Randy could sense the doubt and fear they were having, and he just began to sing what Jackson Randolph had written in his book.

Standing On A Mountain Top

"I stand on a mountaintop with peace in my heart, the joy of knowing the Lord is standing with me as I soar like an eagle across the sky with the grace of God carrying me. The peace that passes all understanding keeps my eyes on the Lord, renewing my mind by being washed in the word daily.
I stand on a mountaintop with peace in my heart, the joy of knowing the Lord is standing with me. The storms are raging all across this land. The world is falling into the enemy's hands. By the grace of God, his children stand on the word of God.
I stand on a mountaintop with peace in my heart, the joy of knowing the Lord is standing with me.
The world cries out to fill the emptiness they are feeling. Call upon the Lord, repenting and turn from the sin and let their hearts fill with forgiveness and peace, the joy of knowing the Lord is standing with them on a mountaintop.
All you have to do is believe your heart is crying for you to accept the Lord standing with you on the mountain top of grace and peace. Oh, LORD, fill this place with your peace and everlasting grace as we stand here on this mountaintop."

They stood listening to this young child sing the song over and over and they saw the beauty within him that radiated the peace and joy of praising the Lord. They began to sing. The messengers on the Island of Reconciliation began to sing with them and across the island their voices of praise to the Lord began to be heard. They believed the song, provided by God for his Glory for the weak, was for them to know he was their strength in time of need and trouble.

Randolph Grant rode his guard for a battle. They were hearing the praise to the Lord in their hearts, and they began to sing along as well. The strength of the LORD was riding with them, and they continued their way to the false palace that would be destroyed by the time they had left with those they came to bring back.

Randolph Grant was met by Silas and his squirrels who would lead them to the routes that were safe to travel.

Silas flew into his arms saying, "For what we can see the palace hasn't been taken or captured."

Randolph Grant said to Silas, "Rumple."

Silas just stared at him and said, "What is rumple?"

Randolph Grant said, "If you were Silas you would know?"

The false squirrel disintegrated in front of everyone. Randolph Grant wondered where his friend was. They continued their journey on the path they had originally started. As the time passed, Randolph Grant prayed that all would go well with everyone being kept safe.

Michael appeared to him and said, "Be of good cheer Randolph Grant. Everyone is in place and there will be victory here today for the Glory of God."

Randolph Grant's guard arrived early in the morning in large numbers. They waited outside the false palace, out of distance of arrows, waiting for the signal that the barrier had been broken by the Bennet and Alistair castles crashing to the ground. Then the attack on the false palace would commence.

They watched as Wilford, at the top of the palace, had Thaddeus Grant, Benjamin, Commander Daniel, guards Oliver, Gavin, Thomas, Alexander, and Ethan placed on the top edge of the palace with what appeared to be with their hands bound behind their backs. Wilford stood smiling and laughing.

A small handful of riders from the palace rode out to Randolph Grant. A palace guard came with a message from Wilford: If Randolph Grant and his guard leave within the hour then Thaddeus Grant and the others would be spared. Otherwise, he would begin pushing them off the edge one at a time.

Randolph Grant looked at each of the riders from the palace and said, "I recognize all of you. Every one of you that stands here before us dropped your sword and left the field with honor. Now to you stand before us with dishonor, we will not leave, however; every one of you can regain your honor by dropping your swords and walking away from this battle that you cannot win."

The riders all turned and rode back to the palace with one stopping. He turned and looked back at Randolph Grant, unmounted his horse, and dropped his sword and was immediately arrested by the palace guard.

His commander, Jack, asked, "Randolph Grant what would be the signal before we can take this palace and those that stand against us."

Randolph Grant looked at his commander and said, "When the palace of Alistair is destroyed then we will charge."

His commander replied, "They are all my friends."

Randolph Grant said to his commander, "They will not fall from the edge. Bow your head, but let your eyes look to the sky for their rescue to come. John are you ready?"

John, who had been injured by the estate guards, replied, "Yes sir."

While the commander bowed his head, looking into the sky, David's eagles were approaching for the rescue.

Randolph Grant said, "John, advance."

John's archers stepped forward as the eagles lifted Thaddeus Grant and everyone off the edge, flying them to safety.

Wilford ordered his archers, "Kill them!"

John's archers shot their arrows and Wilford's archers fell becoming no more. The eagles landed them. They were given swords and horses.

Thaddeus Grant joined Randolph Grant at the front of the line and said, "What took you so long?"

Randolph Grant smiled, laughing with him, and said, "We had to clean a dusty room."

Laughing, Thaddeus Grant replied, "We saw where it was dumped."

Randolph Grant told Thaddeus that they were just waiting for Alistair's Castle to be destroyed and then Wilford would not know what hit him.

Within moments everyone could hear the loud noise of the Alistair Castle and Bennet's Castle being destroyed.

Randolph Grant ordered, "Charge."

The wolves were running to secure the outer palace making sure no palace guards escaped from inside. Ranulf Grant's Army rode through the tunnels entering the palace sweeping the upper and lower levels. Gunnar and Ashlyn Guardians Army of messengers were riding on the Islands of Redemption. The palace guards from Courageous Mountains were covering the backside of the false palace to stop any retreat.

The battle was over within a short time as the enemy surrendered. Wilford was brought to the field and standing before him was Randolph Grant.

Wilford then said, "I guess you are now going to tell me to leave your island that is actually my island." He laughed. "Well, go ahead tell me to leave and I will return and claim them back on another day."

Randolph Grant said, "I have no intentions of telling you to leave the island as he drew his sword. I plan on to sending you back to the hell from which you came."

The guard who laid down his sword shot an arrow into Randolph Grant while Wilford laughed. David, the eagle, picked up the guard and flew high into the clouds before dropping him to his death.

Randolph Grant dropped to one knee,

Thaddeus Grant yelled, "NO!"

Thaddeus ran to him as Randolph fell to the ground. He picked him up in his arms and held him. Tears began to fall from his eyes.

Thaddeus Grant Island Of Reconciliation

Randolph Grant said, "Thaddeus Grant my sword." He whispered into Thaddeus Grant's ear. "Tell him my real name from the world I am from and then end this. His eyes closed and he went limp in Thaddeus Grant's arms."

Thaddeus Grant clutched him in his arms. Tears of love flowed from his eyes for the son he never had and loved with all his heart.

Wilford laughed and boasted that, "I am a Castellan of the Island of Deception, and my lands are many. This island of land you call the Island of Reconciliation is mine and all its lands. I claimed them in your time of Ranulf Everald who I severely injured on this same battlefield destroying his army."

Thaddeus Grant turned and looked at Wilford who smiled and laughed.

"Did you really think a boy whom you named Jackson Randolph could defeat me? I am a Castellan from the Island of Deception." He continued to laugh.

Thaddeus glared at the sword that lay on the ground.

Wilford boasted louder, "The sword you stare at cannot hurt me. It is the same sword that Ranulf brought to the battlefield." Laughing, he continued, "It did him no good and will do you no good either." He giggled with a smirking grin.

Thaddeus Grant reached down, grasped the sword with a tight grip picked it up with tears in his eyes and a fervent authority in his heart walked towards Wilford. "His name was RANDOLPH EVERARD."

The sword's shinning brightness of purity spoke the truth of God. "THE TRUTH SHALL SET YOU FREE"

He held in his hands a True Sword of the Grants with the power of the Word of God.

Fear gripped Wilford, and he tried to run and get away. Daniel and Jack, the commanders, grabbed him. Thaddeus Grant thrust the sword into Wilford who disintegrated, and the wind blew the vaporizing smoke away.

Thaddeus Grant turned to look at Randolph Grant, fell to his knees, cried, and said, "It has been ended, my son."

The wolves Alexander, Randson, and Snowy all gathered around their friend and laid down beside him. The eagles circled him. Silas ran to his friend and hugged his neck.

David said to his animals, "Friends we need to fly him now to the gatehouse of Gideon," They lifted him and took flight and flew him to the Gatehouse of Gideon where his castle awaited him and where he would rest until the trumpets of Gideon would be blown, needing his assistance.

Silas, his friend, still hugged his neck as they flew away from the false palace. When they were a far distance away, Silas said, "STOP! He is alive, he is saying something. Silas leaned over to hear what Randolph Grant was saying.

Silas repeated it as Randolph Grant spoke the words, "Take me back to the false palace the arrow in me cannot reach the Gatehouse of Gideon. Take me back the Sword of Truth must touch the arrow to end the Castellan reign of deception.

The eagles changed course to fly him back to the false palace. The arrow began moving trying to dislodge and work itself free from Randolph Grant for it knew its days were numbered.

Randolph Grant said, "Do not touch the arrow. It must be touched by the Sword of Truth.

While Thaddeus Grant was being comforted by Benjamin, Benji, and the guards, Michael appeared to Thaddeus Grant and said, "Be of good cheer. Thaddeus Grant he will recover and is on his way back to the false palace. The arrow that is in him must be touched with the Sword of Truth for it contains particles of the Castellan. For if others touch it, the Castellan reign will continue through the unexpected ones who touch the arrow.

Thaddeus Grant, still holding the Sword of Truth, looked into the sky and saw the eagles bringing Randolph Grant back and laying him on the ground. Thaddeus Grant touched the arrow with the Sword of Truth, and it became a vapor of smoke blown away by the wind. This ended the reign of deception of Castellan (Wilford), Deceiver (Alistair), and Disruptor (Ambrose).

Michael set forth what needed to be done before the false palace could be destroyed by the messengers. Randolph Grant, Benji, and a physician were taken to the Wolf Mountains so he could be attended to before they would leave to return to the rightful palace

Thaddeus Grant gathered all of his writings that he had kept separate. His staff that he and Benjamin had chosen and their families, the guards of Randolph Grant, Daniel and his officers, the guards who Pastor Dumpling and Randolph Grant led to the Lord and those who are truly in service to Thaddeus Grant. All others were sent to the Airdrocks field to stand, and the armies of the Grants would sweep across the field and all surrounding areas of Airdrocks Valley. Those that remain would return with everyone as well.

The armies of the Grants swept across the field and surrounding areas, and many were still standing on the field and coming from the surrounding areas of the Airdrocks Valley for their hearts were right with God.

Silas and the squirrels left to make secure the safest route to return to the rightful palace of the Grants. When everyone was a safe distance from the false palace Michael's messengers destroyed the false palace and everything associated with it. They crushed the false palace to powder and a mighty gushing wind blew it off and away from the Island of Reconciliation and the Islands of Redemption.

There were new trees and flowers planted in the Valley and the name of the Valley was changed from Airdrocks Valley to the Valley of Daphna which means Victory. Returning to the rightful Grant Palace, Randolph Grant was unconscious. Thaddeus Grant's physician had given him something to cause him to sleep.

Randolph Grant was unable, because of his wound, to announce Randy as Evan Randolph Grant. So, the honor fell to Thaddeus Grant. He announced Randy as Evan Randolph Grant.

In attendance were Thaddeus Grant, Randolph Grant, Benjamin, Benji, Mr. Habens, Kathryn, Pastor Albert Dumpling, William, James, Samuel, Severin, Commander Daniel, and Commander Jack.

Michael made known to Thaddeus Grant, Randolph Grants wish for Pastor Dumpling to be able to be in attendance to see and hear his son Randy be announced. Thaddeus Grant was agreeable because Pastor Dumpling was a new creature in Christ Jesus and the old had been washed away. The Island of Reconciliation was at Peace and the Islands of Redemption were freed as Gunnar was given Swords of Truth to place on each of the islands where the truth of the Word would be spoken to all who came to visit the islands. Ranulf Grant returned to his castle at the Gatehouse of Gideon where he was able to rest with peace.

WHERE THE WORD OF GOD IS SPOKEN THE LIGHT OF THE LORD SHINES - THE DARKNESS RUNS AND HIDES.

&PILOGUE

&veryone was back at the rightful Grant Palace although there was concern for Randolph Grant because of the wound he sustained. He is being cared for. Thaddeus Grant was in awe when first entering the Grants Tower. When he is not taking care of everyday matters for the Island of Reconciliation, checking in on Randolph Grant, he spends quite a lot of time visiting the Grant Tower and seeing the excitement on Evan Randolph Grant's (who still likes to be called Randy) face for all the adventures that await him while he seeks answers and prays for his Mr. Grant for a mysterious ways prayer for healing. He has understood the importance of his calling to be a Grant.

Randolph Grant did keep to his word by placing Uncle Terry in the stocks and allowing all the children to give him a good swat on the behind with a hard loaf of bread baked by Benji. He still was unable to sit for quite some time.

Afterward Thaddeus Grant said, "Randy now that your Uncle Terry is unable to sit for a while, you are going to receive your first responsibility as a Grant. You need to decide what is to be done with Uncle Terry. Remember he did apologize immensely for how he treated you and others in the village."

Randy informed his Uncle Terry that they did have need of an important position that needed to be filled so he gave him Mr. Habens old position at the pier to let everyone know how to come to the Island of Reconciliation. Randy and Steven became great friends. So much that he selected Mr. Habens and Steven for his historians. Terry Teetson Jr hasn't put down the Bible since opening it and became Pastor Dumplings first mentored on becoming a Pastor one day. Jonathan has a crew working on the vision of improvements that Randolph Grant had laid out for the Grants Palace and Burt Teetson has become a trusted friend and helper to him.

God works in mysterious ways.

On Terry's first day at the pier, a group inquired on how to get to the Island of Reconciliation. Terry informed them they would need to have faith and pointed to the end of the pier. In a serious voice he said, "You can take a step of faith, rent a carriage and take a ride of faith, or you could take a dive of faith that water that looks really cool on this hot day."

"Uncle Terry, that's not nice. Bring him to the great hall." Said Evan Randolph Grant as he stood on the Bridge of Reconciliation watching his Uncle Terry, while visitors were landing on the bridge in dives of bruises.

"Michael I am done with the Epilogue report for all the wonderful readers of *Thaddeus Grant Island of Reconciliation*. I am signing off now. Wait a minute, I am a talking squirrel not a writing squirrel. Michael, I need for you to write my name on the report."

Signed Silas, The Smart Red Squirrel

"I signed your name to the Epilogue report Silas," Said, Michael the Messenger. "Oh, here is your bag of treats enjoy."

ACKNOWLEDGMENTS

I want to thank first and foremost Jesus Christ my Lord for opening the door of opportunity to write Thaddeus Grant Island of Reconciliation.

My friend and Pastor, Philip D. Bliss, who was the conduit God used in helping me to step out in faith with his encouragement to walk through the door. Philip D. Bliss also edited my book which I am greatly grateful for as well. There isn't enough to say about his help through the entire process, He has been an inspiration to me.

I would like to thank Fulcrum Publishing for publishing the book.

My wonderful wife Debbie who has shown great patience in my time spent writing my first novel and for her feedback.

I also want to acknowledge and thank my very close friend, Jeff Martin who has been a great encouragement for me in so many ways.

A group of young people at the Chic-fil-A on Rt. 28, Milford, Ohio who have been a huge blessing to me.

Continue On The Journey

The adventures with Thaddeus, Randolph, and
Evan Randolph Grant

Coming Soon
Forests Of Beauty

Randolph Grant
A Quest For Healing

Randolph Grant's wound that he had suffered in the battle with
Wilford the Castellan of the Avenskerri perplexed Dr. Dumpling.
The wound was healing, but Randolph Grant was not. A
persistent fever with chills, unbearable pain that he would
scream ordering everyone to leave the room. When he was alone
the fever would subside, and the pain would be non-existent, but
the thoughts running through his mind would not allow for a
restful sleep. Nightmares would wake him in the night with
panic attacks, recurring dreams that didn't make sense. He was
being tormented but what was causing it and why? Thaddeus
Grant would sit in his chair crying from the despair over the
ailment of Randolph Grant, his concern was starting to tell as he
was becoming agitated with the littlest things. Unable to sit and
share in fellowship with him.

Thaddeus Grant Island Of Reconciliation

"Michael is there nothing you can do to help him?"
Asked, Thaddeus Grant firmly.
He had no answers for Thaddeus Grant.
Randy's heart was broken, for he was unable to see or be with
Mr. Grant whom he loved. His faithfulness in the Lord Jesus was
unwavering with tears of love he would rise early in the morning
to pray asking God to provide a mysterious way for Mr. Grant's
healing. At midday, he would pray continuing to knock on the
door in prayer, and in the evening before going to sleep with
tears running down his cheeks, he would lift a prayer to the
Father in heaven seeking healing and peace for his Mr. Grant.
The nightmares came with a vengeance and the recurring dreams
were crying louder for help he awoke screaming. The guard's
concern for him came into the room causing him to be in
excruciating pain as he yelled GET OUT! Benji was the first to
come running to his room from the commotion, then Thaddeus
and Benjamin awaken Dr. Dumpling.
"Will this never end?"
Thaddeus Grant said, "Randolph Grant, the guards are sorry
for coming into the room, it was out of concern to rush to your
aid."
"Leave me alone, go away."
Michael appeared in the hallway. "Be of good cheer.
Thaddeus Grant go back to your rooms, and I will sit with him
to find out what the recurring dreams are and the nightmares that
are tormenting him. I have two messenger guards that will stand
at his door should he need assistance. He doesn't seem to be in
pain when we are in the room."
Randolph Grant lay in his room in agony and defeated.
"Be of good cheer Randolph Grant." Said Michael.

"What good cheer do you speak of? Do you have a cure for this pain, nightmares, and dreams that will not go away?"

"You are alive, and a Child of God that is the good cheer. I will sit here with you, share with me the nightmares and recurring dreams, and maybe I will understand them to help you rest. "

Randolph Grant and Michael sit talking about the recurring dreams and nightmares. In time he fell asleep as Michael sat there with him all night knowing what the nightmares and dreams were about. When he awakened in the morning Michael was still sitting there with him.

Michael said, "I am going to have a young messenger Luke come and sit with you, there are two messenger guards in the hallway outside your door for your assistance should you need any. I will return later, and we will talk more."

"Where are you going?"

"I am going to talk to Thaddeus Grant. Everyone is very concerned about you. Would you like for me to tell them anything?"

"Just tell everyone I am sorry for my outburst, especially my guards."

"I will let them know." Michael left the room.

Michael came into the Great Hall and said, "Be of good cheer, Thaddeus Grant, and everyone he will be ok. Randolph Grant wanted me to tell everyone he is sorry for his outburst last night. Especially to his guards. The nightmares and recurring dreams have exhausted him not allowing him to have rest. His recurring dream is of a Forest of Beauty which is the Forest of Battleton. In his dream, there is an Oak tree, solid rock, and a black cloud. The Oak tree is dying, the solid rock is Ranulf

Thaddeus Grant Island Of Reconciliation

Grant's Castle he built around the tree and a black cloud has engulfed it."

Thaddeus Grant asked, "What is the black cloud?"

Michael said, "It is the Evil Princess Ansinathia the sister of Wilford. He called for her assistance, she is who sent the ravens, not Wilford, the dusty book in the room was placed there by her. The black cloud that appeared in the room was her as well, she was not defeated in the room when she left, it finally dawned on her that her army the ravens were no more. She destroyed the book on her leaving, she exploded the book on Wilford's end, she was not happy with him. When you thrust the sword of truth into him, and he disintegrated into a vapor blowing away, she was trapped by Wilford in Ranulf Castle. He is no more; the black cloud is the Evil Princess Ansinathia. She is who took the children from the Forest of Beauty and who is tormenting him with nightmares.…

About The Author

"Phillip R. Evans books are written for entertainment - fantasy adventures with a Christian theme."

Phillip R. Evans is a child of God who loves Jesus. He is the author of Thaddeus Grant Island Of Reconciliation. He had a yearning and desire to write books to point back to Jesus. When the opportunity arose by faith, he stepped through the door.

The journey of adventure and fantasy began with the Grants of the Island Of Reconciliation

He was born and raised in Ohio where he and his wife reside.

ℛECONCILIATION

John 3:16-17 KJV

16 For God so loved the world, that he gave his only begotten Son, that whosoever believeth in him should not perish, but have everlasting life. 17 For God sent not his Son into the world to condemn the world; but that the world through him might be saved.

Acts 3:19

Repent ye therefore, and be converted, that your sins may be blotted out, when the times of refreshing shall come from the presence of the Lord.

Romans 5:10 KJV

10 For if, when we were enemies, we were reconciled to God by the death of his Son, much more, being reconciled, we shall be saved by his life.

2 Corinthians 5:18-19 KJV

18 And all things are of God, who hath reconciled us to himself by Jesus Christ, and hath given to us the ministry of reconciliation; To wit, that God was in Christ, reconciling the world unto himself, not imputing their trespasses unto them; and hath committed unto us the word of reconciliation.

Ephesians 4:32 KJV
32 And be ye kind one to another, tenderhearted, forgiving one another, even as God for Christ's sake hath forgiven you.

Colossians 1:20-22 KJV
And, having made peace through the blood of his cross, by him to reconcile all things unto himself; by him, I say, whether they be things in earth, or things in heaven.

Colossians 3:13 KJV
13 Forbearing one another, and forgiving one another, if any man have a quarrel against any: even as Christ forgave you, so also do ye.

PRE Books
Phillip R. Evans
P.O. Box 33
Goshen, Ohio 45122
www.phillipRevans.com